I084669З

LOVE IN THE WIND

By Ellen Fannon

BOOK ONE IN THE LOVE IN THE WIND
SERIES

ALSO BY ELLEN FANNON

Other People's Children
Save the Date – 3rd Place 2022 Christian Indie Award winner
Don't Bite the Doctor
Honor Thy Father – Episode One
Honor Thy Father —Episode Two

CHAPTER ONE

Ben Parish cupped his hand over his brow to block out the blinding sunlight as he scanned the distant road for Doc Tippins' familiar truck. His mare, Maggie, had been in labor for too long, and his anxiety rose steadily with each passing hour of no results. Whispering Winds Ranch had been struggling since his father's death two years ago, and he couldn't afford to lose this mare. Or the foal, either, for that matter.

A constricting band of worry squeezed his heart with the ever-present thought that he would fail and lose what his father and grandfather had worked so hard for. If only Dave had stuck around to help. But ranching had never been in his brother's blood, and when Dad passed unexpectedly, Dave had taken his chance to move on to other endeavors. Ben didn't begrudge his brother. He knew Dave had only stuck it out at the ranch as long as he did for their father's sake. Still, Ben couldn't help wishing he and Dave could have continued running the ranch together as a family.

A gust of nippy wind assaulted him, and he buttoned up his faded denim jacket with the holes in the sleeves over his old flannel shirt. The cold air stung his reddened cheeks and work-roughened hands, but he didn't want to take the time to look for his gloves. Jamming his hands into his pockets, he paced the distance between the house and the detached garage several yards away, his scuffed boots wearing a deeper rut into the dried mud path.

Ah! Finally. He released the breath he hadn't even realized he'd been holding as the sight of a pickup truck appeared on the isolated road running past the ranch. Doc Tippins would assess the situation with the unproductive birth and soon set everything right. The old veterinarian had been doctoring their animals since Ben was a boy, and the man exuded competence and confidence with his years of experience.

But as the vehicle drew nearer, Ben realized it wasn't Doc Tippins' old blue Ford. Did he get a new truck? The old one had to have a lot of miles on it from driving all over southern Wyoming. Well, good for Doc. He deserved something more modern than that old broken-down rust bucket he had driven for the past twenty years.

The truck turned in at the entrance to Whispering Winds Ranch, the gravel crunching under the tires, and kicking up dust in its wake. A smile of relief tugged at the corners of Ben's lips as he walked forward to meet the only man in three counties who could perform animal miracles. Just as quickly, the smile slipped from his face when he realized it wasn't Doc Tippins at the wheel. Drat. Who was this stranger and what did they want?

A young woman in baggy brown coveralls hopped out of the truck, her chestnut-colored ponytail whipping in the breeze. Her smile seemed forced as she stepped forward, her hand extended.

"Good morning," she greeted. "I'm Dr. Darcy Fuller. I understand you have a mare with dystocia."

Ben's brow now furrowed into a full-blown scowl. Ignoring her outstretched hand, he said, "Where's Doc Tippins?"

The young woman's smile disappeared as she dropped her hand to her side. "He's doing an emergency surgery. I'm his new associate."

Ben's lips flattened as he appraised the girl. She looked like she was no more than eighteen, although if she was a veterinarian, she had to be older. Still, she couldn't have much, if any, experience—probably a new graduate. What was Doc Tippins thinking sending this wet-behind-the-ears newbie to attend to a critical case like his? He tried to swallow his irritation but failed.

Scrubbing his hand over his forehead, where a throbbing headache had suddenly taken root, he closed his eyes and took a deep breath through his nose, blowing it out slowly through his pinched lips.

He opened his eyes and attempted to be pleasant. "Look. I'm sure you can do vaccines and worming and Coggins testing and the like. But for something serious like this, I need Doc Tippins. I've known him for over twenty years and I trust him."

The woman seemed to deflate as she let out a defeated sigh. "I understand. I can try to call Dr. Tippins and see how much longer he will be."

A prickle of compassion tugged at Ben's conscience. This girl, whatever her name was—he had already forgotten it—was probably used to rejection, being the new associate when everyone wanted Doc

Tippins. But still, he didn't know anything about her qualifications, and Maggie's desperate situation required someone with experience whom he could rely on.

"No offense," he said, as she walked back to her truck, her head down and shoulders slumped. He watched as she held a cell phone to her ear, although he couldn't quite make out what she said. Still, it didn't take much imagination to figure out what the discussion entailed. The woman had probably had several similar conversations with her boss about clients preferring to see him rather than her.

After a moment, she got out of the truck again, tucking the cell phone into her back pocket. "He says he should be able to get here within an hour. Would you like me to take a preliminary look at the mare, or do you want to wait for him?"

Ben hesitated. He didn't like hurting her feelings, but what if she caused more trauma to an already precarious condition? No, it was better to wait for the doc. No need to put Maggie through more handling than necessary. He cleared his throat and his eyes fell just short of meeting hers. "Um, no, that's okay. I think it would be better to wait. Again, no offense."

She lowered her chin and nodded. "Okay then. If there's nothing I can do for you, I'll go on to some other calls." This time, she held her head high as she returned to the truck and slid inside. Just before closing her door, she said, "Good luck. I hope your mare is okay."

"Thanks." Ben gave her a half-hearted smile and a wave. Mixed thoughts swirled through his mind as he watched her put the truck in reverse and turn around to head back down the long driveway. Should he have given her a chance? What if Doc Tippins was delayed even longer? Was he taking a risk by waiting? Well, here he was, back at square one. He turned to go check on Maggie.

Tears stung Darcy's eyes as she headed back toward the road. Why was it when someone said, "no offense," they were about to say something offensive? To a degree, she understood the reluctance of the clients to trust her ability when they were used to Dr. Tippins. But sooner or later, they would have to get used to someone else. Dr. Tippins was getting up in age and wouldn't be practicing forever. Part of her reason for coming to the remote area of Baker, Wyoming, had been the incentive to one day take over his practice.

But how was that ever going to happen if no one allowed her to do her job? How was she supposed to prove herself if no one gave her a chance? So far, in the few weeks she'd been here, she'd been met with doubt, hesitation, and downright hostility. Only a handful of clients had been friendly and welcoming.

Why had she moved hundreds of miles away from home to make a fresh start? Maybe she had made a mistake. At the rate she was going, she wasn't even earning her paycheck. Perhaps she should move back home. There, she had contacts. Veterinarians she had worked for in school and after she'd graduated would be happy to take her on as an associate, knowing she was a capable, hard worker.

But if she went back home, she'd have the constant

reminder of Josh. She didn't think she could bear that. Coming to Wyoming had seemed such an adventure, a whole new world where no one knew her and her history. That decision had proved to be a double-edged sword. While having no history had its advantages, it also had its drawbacks when getting to know people, let alone trying to establish herself in a demanding career where trust meant everything.

She'd tried to give the decision to God. She'd prayed repeatedly about the move, and although God hadn't exactly sent a burning bush, she had peace about her decision. But since being in Baker, she wondered if that peace had been a product of her own wishful thinking to escape the small-town wagging tongues back home.

Swiping a finger under her lower lids, she said, "Darcy, you will *not* cry." After all, it took time to get established in a new area. Even Dr. Tippins had to start *somewhere*. She took a faltering breath and, putting the arrogant cowboy out of her mind, drove to her next appointment to pull blood for Coggins testing.

CHAPTER TWO

With the move to Wyoming, Darcy needed to find a new place of worship. Plus, church might be a good place to make new friends—maybe even potential clients. She'd visited a couple of churches in the area but had come away with the same impression. Small towns were tight-knit communities that didn't readily welcome outsiders. Although not unfriendly, nobody actively worked to include her in their conversations, short of a perfunctory welcome and then moving on to greet their friends.

This Sunday, Darcy decided to try a church she had seen on her way to a more remote farm. Although farther from her apartment than the other two churches she had previously attended, she wanted to find a place where she would fit in.

She missed her family and friends back in Pennsylvania. She had enjoyed horseback riding through the Poconos, as well as serving as a veterinarian to many of the area's stables, where she was accepted and respected. But she rarely got a chance to share her history and experience with the Wyoming locals.

Her parents owned Fuller Farms, one of the most

popular riding stables in Caryville, where she'd grown up with horses, leading trail rides and giving riding lessons. Naturally, her parents expected her to stick around and render veterinary services after graduating from Penn State. It was what she had expected also—to live her life happily ensconced in the town where she had grown up, doing the work she had always wanted to do, surrounded by friends and family she had always known. But Josh changed all that. Now, a pang of remorse for leaving her parents' stable after they had helped put her through school jabbed at her heart. But her parents had been supportive and understanding.

Pushing her homesickness to the back of her mind, she turned her truck into a newly paved parking lot in front of the attractive church she had noticed on her rounds. Today she came early to attend Sunday school. Sometimes small groups made it easier to meet people and make friends, although it took every bit of her courage to force herself to walk into yet another body of strangers.

Her stomach rebelled at the coffee she'd swigged during the twenty-minute drive, flip-flopping around in her abdomen as if someone had poked an angry bees' nest. But to become established in this area, she would have to make an effort. People weren't going to come to her when they didn't even know she existed. Although she had met several clients, she didn't have a comradery with any of them yet, outside of a professional relationship. And at the rate her career was going in Baker, becoming chummy with any of the few clients who gave her the benefit of the doubt seemed remote. She missed the friendships she'd had with her clients in Pennsylvania.

Darcy ambled halfway across the parking lot, taking in the rare warmth of the sunshine and the magnificent powder-blue sky with tufts of feathery white clouds. After the cold of the last few weeks, the soft heat from the sun soothed her soul.

She stopped for a moment to close her eyes and immerse herself in the beauty of the day, attuning her senses to the sweet songs of the birds and the scent of wildflowers nearby. Inhaling deeply, still with her eyes closed, she let peace wash over her. Darcy always felt closest to God in nature. As she filled her lungs with clean, pure air, someone rammed into her from behind, knocking the wind out of her.

A hand reached out and steadied her while Darcy fought to regain her balance and catch her breath. Embarrassed, she turned and looked straight into the face of the arrogant cowboy from Whispering Winds Ranch. She had forgotten his name, only remembering him as the arrogant cowboy.

"Are you all right?" He still held on to her arm, sending a surge of heat up to her shoulder and into her neck and cheeks. "I'm so sorry. You just kind of stopped and, well, I guess I wasn't watching where I was going."

Darcy swallowed against the dryness in her throat, her mouth suddenly devoid of meaningful words to speak, her humiliation burning from her head to her toes.

His eyes searched hers, and she became aware of how intensely blue they were—sort of like the glorious sky. She hadn't taken much note of his appearance a few days ago, but then she rarely paid much attention to clients' looks, being more focused on their animals.

"Hey, don't I know you from somewhere?" He finally released her arm and took a step back, his brows bunched together in thought, studying her face. Then he shook his head and chuckled. "I'm not really trying to use an old cliche."

She managed to nod, lowering her eyes from his penetrating gaze. "We met at your ranch. I'm Darcy Fuller."

From his confused look, she knew he still couldn't place her. "*Dr.* Fuller."

A slow recognition moved across his features, and it was his turn to redden. "Oh. Yes." An awkward smile appeared at the corners of his lips, and she derived a small sense of satisfaction that he seemed more uncomfortable than she did. "Um, so . . . how are you?"

She narrowed her eyes at the obligatory polite question. Why did people always ask how you were when all they wanted to hear was, "Fine. How are you?" No one cared to hear about your gall bladder attacks, your financial woes, or your broken heart when they asked that trite question.

Darcy was half tempted to lay into him about her trials and tribulations, as well as the fact that nobody trusted her veterinary abilities, including him. He *had* asked. It would serve him right to be held hostage while she regaled him with her life's troubles. But she was on her way to church, after all. Forgive and forget. Well, forgive, anyway. Besides, she didn't want to hold a grudge against this guy. He was well within his rights to want the very best for his animals, and he didn't know her from Dr. Seuss.

"I'm good. How is your mare?" She'd forgotten to ask her boss how the dystocia had turned out.

His eyes lit up and his initially weak smile stretched across his face. "Everything went fine. She delivered a healthy, beautiful little bay filly with a white star across her forehead. I named her 'Star.' I know 'Star' is not very original, but the name fit her so well I just couldn't help myself."

Darcy's heart thawed a tiny bit as she listened to him describe his new foal with such passion. "I'm glad." Then she couldn't help but ask, "What was the problem with the birth?"

"One of Star's front legs was bent back. After Doc repositioned it, she came with no trouble."

Something I could have easily fixed without the poor mare having to wait an extra hour. Darcy bit her tongue to keep from saying the words aloud. "Good. I'm happy everything worked out well." She averted her eyes. "Um, I guess we should be going in." She took a few steps, not looking to see if he followed.

"Yeah, we should." He caught up to her. "Is this your first time at Aspen Community Church?"

Darcy paused. "Yes. I'm visiting different churches in the area." *And will probably not be coming back here.*

"I can show you to the singles' Sunday school class If you'd like. It's not a big group, but we're all family in the spiritual sense." He stopped. "Oh, I just assumed you were single. We have a young married class, also."

Stabbing pain shot through her gut. "No, I'm single." *Very single.*

Ben led the way to the singles' Sunday school room

in the back of the handsome red-brick church, his boots echoing off the tiled corridor. He cast furtive glances at the young woman by his side as they walked along. He hadn't recognized her at first without her messy ponytail or her baggy brown coveralls—which did nothing to enhance her slim figure or her shapely legs. He had to admit Darcy Fuller cleaned up rather well, with her thick, shoulder-length hair curling softly around her heart-shaped face.

She wore a modest, short-sleeved green dress that brought out the green in her hazel eyes. Not that he had been studying her eyes, but they'd had those few awkward moments in the parking lot while he was trying to place where he had seen her before. It had been hard to tell how pretty she was the other day. But, of course, he hadn't been focused on her looks. Or— chagrin wormed its way into his conscience—her abilities as a veterinarian. He hadn't even given her a chance. He had immediately made a snap judgment that she was too young and inexperienced and dismissed her as being incapable of taking care of Maggie's problem. Ben told himself he was only looking out for Maggie and the foal's best interest, but a nagging little voice in the back of his head told him he had been unfair. At least Darcy went to church. Still, churchgoing didn't automatically equate to good veterinary medicine.

His thoughts were interrupted when they arrived at the singles' Sunday school class, a cozy room in the back corner of the building. Beams of sunlight filtered through the opened Venetian blinds leaving shards of brightness on the dark blue carpet. A half-dozen young people occupying padded chairs placed around the perimeter of the room looked up with curiosity as Ben entered with the newcomer.

"Everyone, this is Darcy Fuller. She's . . ." Ben paused. He really didn't know anything about her, such as where she was from or how long she'd been in the area. He didn't even know if she was a good veterinarian.

Darcy rescued him. "I'm Dr. Tippins' new associate."

"Oh!" A brunette with a pixie haircut hopped out of her chair, grabbed Darcy's hand, and pulled her further into the room. "We're so glad to meet you. Everyone just loves Doc Tippins, but it's time he got some help." She continued leading Darcy toward a chair next to hers and indicated for her to sit, as she kept up a running monologue. "He's always so busy. It's nice that he's got a new, young woman assistant. I'm Molly Lewis, by the way. Next time I need a vet, I'll ask for you."

Ben noticed Darcy didn't correct Molly's mistake of saying "assistant" rather than "associate." Even he knew the difference. But Molly welcomed Darcy with open arms and an open mind, something he'd not done. Several others jumped into the conversation, leaving him with little to say as he stood, suddenly feeling like more of an outsider than Darcy. He slid into a seat across the room and tried to focus on the lesson rather than the attractive young vet who'd unsettled him for reasons he hadn't quite worked out in his mind.

After Sunday school, the lesson of which went completely over Ben's head as his thoughts ran amok through his brain, he debated briefly whether or not to escort Darcy into the sanctuary. But he needn't have been concerned. Molly latched onto Darcy's arm as if they were new best friends and led her out, gabbing away as if she had known Darcy all her life. Darcy didn't even spare a glance in Ben's direction. Okay, so his responsibility toward showing her hospitality was finished. He should have felt relieved to be free of further duty. Instead, an unexpected, unexplained twinge of annoyance crept over him at Molly for having commandeered his charge.

He chided himself over his inexplicable feelings and headed to the sanctuary, where he took a seat several rows behind and to the right of the two women, whose heads were bent together in animated conversation. Why should he care? Darcy probably didn't have many friends in town and Molly was warm and gregarious. But Molly had always struck him as an "over-the-top" extrovert who, frankly, made him want to escape whenever she cornered him. Her "Energizer Bunny" energy wore him out. He wondered, fleetingly, if she was wearing Darcy out, too, and Darcy might be wishing to be rescued. Then he caught Darcy's unrestrained laugh and decided she could handle herself. Again, why did he even care? He delved into studying the bulletin as the organist began the prelude.

At the end of the service, several members of the singles' class converged on him asking if he was going to lunch today, as they usually did after worship. For some reason, he caught Darcy's eye and murmured, "Not today. I've got a lot of work to do."

"Come on, Ben," said Molly, "you always go out with the group."

He averted his eyes. "Sorry. I can't." Then he turned and walked quickly away.

Molly put her hands on her hips and stared after him. "What's got into him? He acts like somebody kicked his dog." Then she laughed. "Sorry, poor choice of words considering you're a vet."

Darcy compressed her lips. "I think it's my fault. He doesn't like me."

Molly raised her eyebrows. "Why shouldn't he like you? Ben's friendly to everyone."

The others in the little group looked on with interest. Darcy sighed. "I went out to his ranch a few days ago on a call. He was not happy I wasn't Dr. Tippins. He wouldn't even let me examine his mare." She realized her tone had become more bitter than she'd intended but she continued. "In fact, he was rather rude and condescending."

Molly waved Darcy's comments aside. "Things will change once he gets to know you."

Darcy wasn't sure she wanted to get to know Ben. Still, he had been courteous after plowing into her in the parking lot. He'd shown her to the Sunday school room and introduced her—an introduction that had, more or less, been thrust upon him since they had walked in together. And, now that she thought about it, it wasn't much of an introduction. He had choked on her name, and she'd had to finish introducing herself. But, to be honest, he wouldn't have been put in the position of escorting her into the church if she hadn't stopped dead in the middle of the parking lot, even if she was trying to infuse herself with the courage to walk in. She'd gotten a little distracted by the beautiful day God had made.

"Well, you're coming to lunch with us," Molly

announced, leaving no room for argument. "Come on, you're riding with me."

Darcy found she was grateful for the other woman's outgoing, friendly—if a little bossy—nature and gladly accepted.

The group managed to find a table for five at Francine's, a popular locally-owned café.

"Looks like we finally beat the Methodists to lunch," said a short, cheerful young man sitting next to Darcy whose name she couldn't remember.

"This place is crowded," Darcy said, looking around. "The food here must be good." The enticing aromas wafting through the room reminded her of how hungry she was. Now that the unsettling churning in her stomach had dissipated with Ben's absence, she sat back and relaxed, eager to try out a new restaurant and get to know her new friends.

Molly, sitting on Darcy's other side, placed a hand on her arm and said, "Yes, it is. But mostly we love this place because of Francine, the owner. She's been running this place forever, and everybody loves her." Frown lines formed across her forehead. "That's another reason I'm surprised Ben didn't come. Francine is like a second mother to him."

Great, we're back on the topic of Ben.

Molly leaned over in a conspiratorial manner to fill Darcy in. "Ben's mom died of cancer when he was a teenager. Francine practically helped raise him and his brother, Dave, after that." Although Molly's head bent close to Darcy's ear, and she spoke in a soft tone, the words were picked up by the rest of the group, whose tongues clucked in sympathy.

"Everyone thought she and Ben's dad might end up

together," confided a red-headed woman across the table, another person whose name Darcy couldn't remember.

"That family's had one setback after another," said the sandy-haired man on Molly's other side, whom Darcy remembered as Tim.

Great! Darcy knew two of the four names of the people at the table. She hoped someone would let a name slip so she didn't have to embarrass herself by asking.

Molly sighed. "It took Justin, Ben's dad, a long time to get over losing his wife. Then Justin died of a heart attack out of the blue. Nobody expected a fatal heart attack to happen to someone so young and fit."

"And Dave left Ben to take care of everything on his own," said Redhead.

Heads turned right and left as each person took up the story.

"Then those two freak storms, back-to-back that caused all that damage and wiped out a number of his cattle . . ."

"And the problem with the insurance . . ."

"Ben's had a rough time trying to hold that ranch together . . ."

"And then that whole situation with Jolene . . ."

They weren't exactly gossiping, but the hot topic of Ben's life provided a wealth of unsolicited information for Darcy's brain. Obviously, the guy had problems she'd been unaware of. Perhaps she needed to cut the guy a little slack. She'd been so busy feeling sorry for herself, that she hadn't considered anyone else's difficulties. A sliver of regret for her hasty judgment of the man as an arrogant cowboy lodged in her chest.

Thank goodness she hadn't uttered her opinion aloud. And, despite all of Ben's misfortunes, he went to church, which said something about his character.

"He's such a good-looking man, too . . ." That was Molly, regret filling her tone.

"Well, why don't you two get together?" Redhead. She narrowed her eyes and grinned. "I know you want to."

Darcy risked a sideways peek at Molly. "Oh, you know," Molly replied, batting away the question with her hand, "we're not right for each other."

Redhead snorted. "Neither was Jolene, but that didn't stop him."

"Jolene." Molly rolled her eyes. "But you know who would be perfect for him?" Molly stopped and turned to Darcy. "A pretty, young lady veterinarian."

All eyes landed on Darcy, as her jaw dropped and heat flamed her face.

The conversation continued to buzz around Darcy, but still reeling from what Molly had said, the words became blurred. Fortunately, the waitress arrived to take their orders, interrupting the saga of Ben and further speculation of how perfect she would be for him. Of all the crazy ideas! By the time the waitress left, the conversation moved on to other areas, and finally to just Darcy, with everyone wanting to know about her. By the end of the meal, Darcy had four new friends and three new clients.

CHAPTER THREE

When Ben pulled out of the church parking lot, he felt left out of his own young adults' group. He shook his head. That was ridiculous. He'd been invited to lunch just like every other Sunday. He'd been the one who turned the situation weird by refusing to go, simply because of *her*. What was he, in junior high school? He drummed his fingers on the steering wheel for a moment, debating whether or not to change his mind and go on to Francine's, the restaurant they generally frequented. Then he decided to skip it. He didn't want to make Darcy uncomfortable.

The next day, Ben kept busy, trying to keep his mind on the ranch. It seemed like just when he had one thing fixed, another problem crept up. Everything seemed to fall apart after his dad's unexpected death. First, those storms that had left fences down, and buildings and equipment damaged, not to mention several dead Angus cattle. Ben worked feverishly to deal with the aftermath of those disasters.

It was then he learned the dire financial situation of

the ranch. His father had never said a word to him or Dave, but they had been barely breaking even for several years. Certain things had to go, and one of those things was the extensive insurance on the property and livestock. They'd never had a major claim, and apparently, Justin Parish couldn't justify the insurance expense with the money stretching only so far. He'd replaced the policy with a cheaper one.

The loss of the cattle, which had been almost ready to take to auction, on top of everything else, had nearly put the ranch into bankruptcy. Ben took out a loan and slowly worked to rebuild, but it was like treading mud. Even minor setbacks, as were inevitable in this line of work, became major headaches. He'd bought some replacement cows, many of them already pregnant, which had seemed like a good idea at the time.

But now, on top of everything else, he had several calves— from the new cows—sick with diarrhea. He isolated the affected animals, moving them into an easily disinfected section of the barn, and supplemented them with extra colostrum and electrolytes. He had even gone to the feed store and bought some antibiotics that were supposed to be good for intestinal disorders, but the medication hadn't done much good. He'd also tried some oral vaccines because he was becoming suspicious that the new cattle had not been vaccinated, despite the seller's assurance to the contrary. The reliable source from whom they usually got replacement cattle had been sold, and maybe the new operation didn't have the same high-quality standards. But how was he to know? Maybe he should have asked around first, but at the time, he didn't think much about using the same facility they'd always used.

If only his father were here. Dad always had a gift with sick animals. He should have gone to veterinary school. But he preferred ranching and he was a good rancher. At least until Mom died. Then he'd kind of let things go. By the time Dad managed to dig himself out of his dark place, the ranch had suffered financial blows, from which Ben was desperately trying to extricate himself. But sometimes he felt like just giving up and selling out. Then what would he do? That thought alone kept him struggling to turn the ranch around and make it profitable again because he didn't know what else he could do to earn a living.

Ben's shoulders slumped when the stench of more diarrhea greeted him upon entering the barn. His boots scraped across the straw to the isolation area where he'd confined nine sick calves. He assessed the animals over the waist-high gate. At least they were still standing and their eyes seemed relatively bright. But feces soiled the rear ends of several of the beasts.

Letting out a sigh, Ben herded them into the next stall before grabbing a pitchfork and mucking out the dirtied straw. After thoroughly cleaning and disinfecting the concrete floor, he offered milk and electrolytes to the group, relieved to see that most of them readily drank. But he had to drench the three who refused.

After preparing the fluids, he lubricated the end of a stomach tube. Grabbing the first calf, he pressed it up against his leg, restrained its head, and pulled its tongue to the side, deftly sliding the tube down the side of its mouth. The calf didn't put up much of a fight, swallowing easily as the tube reached the larynx. Ben advanced the tube into the rumen and administered the fluids, then kinked the tube so as not to dribble any liquid into the trachea as he pulled it out. He repeated the process with the other two, thankful that neither gave him much resistance. But, on the other hand, lack of resistance also meant a lack of strength to fight. He would have to watch these three closely. Maybe when he went into town later today, he would stop in at Doc Tippins' clinic and see if he had anything better to treat them with.

Ben fetched a bucket of warm water, soap, and clean towels, and washed the caked feces from all the affected calves to prevent fecal scald. Then he pitched fresh hay into the pen he'd just cleaned.

"Come on, guys, give me a break and get better." He stood looking at them for a moment as if by sheer willpower he could make them cooperate and get over whatever was making them sick. Then he shot up a quick prayer that no more calves would get sick

Darcy was gathering supplies for her afternoon calls when she heard the door to the clinic open. She didn't pay much attention until she heard *his* voice in the reception area.

"Afternoon, Pam. Is Doc Tippins around?"

The receptionist answered, "No, I'm afraid not, Ben. He's been out all day. But Doc Fuller is still here."

Darcy held her breath and tiptoed closer to the lobby so she could hear better. She wished she could see his expression. But she figured his face registered disappointment and possibly annoyance. She didn't hear any more talking, so she risked peeking around the corner. To her surprise, the arrogant cowboy—okay, she really needed to stop thinking of him in that way—sported a slight smile, the corners of his lips turning up slightly, his cheeks flushed with splotches of red. Darcy drew her head back, leaned against the wall, and waited.

"Would you like me to see if she's available?" Pam asked.

Pam's question was answered by the sound of a male clearing his throat. "Uh . . . yeah, I guess. I just need a minute, if it's not too much trouble. I mean, I wouldn't want to interrupt if she's doing something important."

"Let me check."

Darcy tried to back-peddle as Pam came barreling through the doorway, nearly running into her. Darcy really needed to stop putting herself in people's direct paths, or she was going to end up knocked on her keister.

Pam stopped abruptly and grinned. "If you're not busy, Dr. Fuller," she said, a hint of amusement in her voice, "Ben Parish would like a minute."

Busted! Darcy bit her lip and winced. "Thank you, Pam. Send him back." She tried to compose herself while quickly looking around for something to make herself look busy.

As she heard his boots on the tile floor, Darcy quickly snatched her bag and pretended to be searching through the contents. She glanced up as the boots stopped directly in front of her, heat infusing her face as she looked into those blue eyes. Her gaze settled on him just a few seconds too long. *Oh good grief, why am I blushing?* Probably because of what Molly said yesterday.

"Dr. Fuller, I hope I'm not disrupting your schedule."

She almost snorted at the idea of his disrupting all two of her afternoon appointments. "No, no, not at all. I was just getting ready to go on a couple of routine calls. Come on back into the treatment area." Darcy turned to lead the way, then figured he probably knew the clinic better than she did. "And please. Call me Darcy." They moved into the large treatment room, where Darcy leaned against the cabinets and folded her arms across her chest. "What can I do for you?"

He took off his Stetson and ran his hand through unruly dark hair. "I was wondering if you have something effective for calf scours for calves between two and three weeks old. I seem to remember Doc had a powder we used a while back."

"Calf scours?" Thankfully, her professionalism took over. "I'm sorry to hear that. How long has it been going on?"

Ben's fingers worried the brim of his hat. "A few days. I've tried the stuff from the feed store. I'm still giving them colostrum, and even gave them some antibiotics and an oral vaccine."

Darcy bit her lip. He had been a rancher longer than she had been a vet. Would he trust her advice? Or did he just want to get Doc's powder and get out of there? Throwing caution to the wind, she plowed ahead. He could take her advice for what it was worth or leave it.

"I'm afraid the oral vaccines given to calves to prevent viral diarrhea have not proven to be very effective. The vaccine virus is inactivated by antibodies in the colostrum. Besides, it wouldn't help after the disease is already present. The best preventive medicine is to vaccinate the dry cows."

"Yes, I know. I was assured they had been vaccinated when I bought them, but now I'm having my doubts."

Again, Darcy hesitated, but she didn't want to risk offending him by suggesting he should have verified the vaccination status. Anyway, it might not be viral diarrhea. It could be a number of other possibilities. "Well, there are other causes of calf diarrhea besides viruses. if you'd like, I can check for parasites and send samples for testing of other organisms."

He pondered a moment. "How expensive would that be?"

"Checking for parasites is pretty inexpensive, but running cultures or titers could run into a few hundred dollars."

He winced, and she remembered the conversation at lunch in which the group had alluded to Ben having financial difficulties.

Without meeting her eyes, he mumbled, "Do you have any other suggestions?"

She took a deep breath. Whatever she said at this point was critical and might make or break his fledgling trust in her. She knew how hard this must be for him to take the initiative and ask for her advice.

"Have you lost any animals?"

He shook his head. "No, thank goodness. Not yet."

"How sick are they? Are they drinking on their own?"

"Six are. Three aren't. I'm having to drench them. But they've remained alert."

"What else have you done so far?"

He searched the ceiling as if the answer might be up there. Then he ran his hand through his hair again. "I've brought the sick ones into an area of the barn where I can isolate and treat them. I clean and disinfect the stalls at least two or three times a day. I clean the feces from their rear ends so they don't get irritated."

She nodded, considering her response given his economic position. "Well, at this point, I'd hold off running tests unless you lose an animal. If that happens, I would recommend a full necropsy and submission of samples. Continue the colostrum and the electrolyte supplementation. I'll get you some of the supplement we carry. I believe it's better than what you can buy over the counter. I wouldn't recommend any more antibiotics, as that could potentially complicate the problem. Continue with the good nursing care, cleaning, and disinfecting." She then added, "Of course, if you'd like to get Dr. Tippins' opinion, I can have him call you later."

His look of surprise at her last statement caught her unaware. He seemed to be considering whether or not she had made the offer as a taunt for how he had treated her at the ranch.

"No, I'm sure what you've told me is the best course of action."

An awkward moment passed. Finally, she said, "Okay, then. I'll go grab you some electrolyte powder." She escaped his wounded gaze and disappeared into the supply room.

When she returned, bearing a plastic bag with several pouches inside, he said, "Look, about the other day—"

"It's okay," she said, brushing aside what she knew

he was about to say.

He frowned and took a step toward her. "No, it's not okay. I was rude and—"

Once again, she cut him off. "I understand. You were worried about your mare. You don't know me."

He flattened his lips and blew a slow breath out between them. "Still, I apologize." He held out his hand.

Darcy hesitated, then grasped his calloused hand in hers, unprepared for the tingling sensation that swept up her arm.

"Apology accepted," she said, feeling the stupid heat in her cheeks again. Abruptly, she pulled her hand away and thrust the bag into his still outstretched hand. Avoiding his eyes, she muttered, "Try this. Hopefully, it will help."

"Thanks," he said, his voice soft. "And thanks for your help." He seemed to want to say more, but he turned, placed his hat on his head, and moved for the lobby. Once he had reached the front desk, he stopped and looked back to where she still stood. "Darcy?"

"Yes?" She walked into the lobby.

"It was good to see you at church. I hope you'll come again on Sunday."

Darcy felt a smile tugging at her lips. "Thank you. I might. And thanks for showing me around."

He tipped his hat. "My pleasure."

The smile stayed on Darcy's face as the cowboy— not so arrogant, after all—continued to study her.

"Shall I put this on your bill, Ben?" asked Pam, interrupting his staring.

"Yes, please." He shot Darcy one more backward glance and headed out the door.

"*Darcy*? What is this *Darcy* business?" asked Pam, playful mocking coloring her tone.

Darcy scowled. "It's nothing. Just being friendly, that's all." She turned on her heel to finish packing up her supplies.

"Yeah, if I were ten years younger, I wouldn't mind being friendly with Ben Parish," Pam called after her.

CHAPTER FOUR

Ben drove away from the clinic, surprised to realize he had a grin on his face.

What are you grinning like an idiot for, Parish? He forced the smile from his face, only to feel it returning. All-in-all, the impromptu meeting with the pretty, new vet hadn't gone too badly. Once again, she sported her baggy, brown coveralls, and her hair had been pulled back into a ponytail—although not quite as messy as the other day. But she exuded warmth and caring and, he had to admit, she seemed knowledgeable.

He still felt bad about jumping to conclusions about her the first time they'd met. Plus, she went to church, a distinct positive in her favor. He figured she was church shopping and hoped she'd come back, although her first two encounters with him hadn't been all that welcoming. First, he'd run her off his ranch, then he'd bailed on going to lunch, making a total donkey's patoot out of himself. Still, he'd minded his manners today. He'd even apologized for his boorish behavior. But sometimes you couldn't close the barn door once the horse was out.

What was it about this woman that made her opinion of him so important? Well, besides the fact that they would inevitably be thrown together in a professional capacity, as Doc Tippins couldn't be everywhere at once, and was nearing retirement age. Ben certainly didn't want her to think of him as one of those difficult clients she dreaded seeing.

But something about her tugged at his closed-off heart. Why, exactly, he didn't know. He barely knew Darcy. Besides, he'd vowed two years ago, after Jolene, never to get involved with a woman again. And he had kept that vow. Her betrayal had been too painful, and in his love-blinded state, he had never seen it coming. In retrospect, there had been several red flags, her disinterest in attending church being a huge one. He knew what the Bible said about being unequally yoked, but he figured they could work out their differences when it came to their faith after they were married. But his shattered heart couldn't go through that anguish again. His heart was now barely held together with scar tissue covering the holes. If it broke again, it would never heal. Several women had tried to help him forget Jolene, but he'd held them all at arm's length.

He was better off staying unattached, not putting himself out there for his heart to be crushed again. And until now, it had been easy. So why did his mind not want to let go of the intriguing new vet? It wasn't just because she was pretty. Lots of pretty women had thrown themselves at him. It also wasn't because he felt guilty for the way he had treated her—twice. But underneath that professional persona, he could tell she was genuine, although how he knew that, he couldn't say—and he warned himself to be careful. He had thought Jolene was genuine, too. He also sensed a certain vulnerability about Darcy. Maybe she'd had some pain in her past that had left scars like his. Come to think of it, why had she moved to a strange place all alone? Was she running away from something, or someone?

He shook his head, as if that would clear the image of her from his brain, and thought about all the work that awaited him at home. Besides having sick calves to attend to, he had to check the rest of the herd to look for any newly ill animals. He needed to start work on the barn roof. After the last storm, he'd lost several shingles, and there had been some leaks. The roof needed to be fixed before it rained again, especially with sick calves inside. He also had repairs to make on the fence. The fence always needed mending. He couldn't afford for his cattle to wander loose off the property. The house was in desperate need of a new coat of paint, but that would have to wait.

Sometimes the never-ending work seemed overwhelming. When Dad was alive, they'd had lots of hired hands to help with all the work. But with money so tight, Ben had had to let several men go, which only increased his workload. Still, there had been no choice. He couldn't pay what he didn't have.

Ben pulled into his long driveway, noting with a sinking feeling in his gut that the truck was making a new noise. Add one more thing to his to-do list. He shut off the engine, grabbed his purchases from town, and strode to the house. The old wooden boards of the porch creaked in protest under his boots. Replacing those boards before someone fell through and broke a leg had also long been on his intended agenda.

Sighing, he unlocked the door and walked into the kitchen, dumping his bags on the table. A leaky faucet dripping on the dirty dishes he'd left in the sink caught his attention. Swell. Then he heard the beep of the answering machine, indicating he had messages. He walked over to the house phone on the opposite kitchen counter and pushed play. He would like to get rid of the house phone and the phone bill, but sometimes cell service was spotty out here. The tinny, electronic voice on the machine told him he had one new message. He listened as the machine announced the day and time of the message before the familiar voice of Lance Marshall, his loan officer and former high school classmate, filled the room.

"Ben, this is Lance Marshall from First City Bank. I'm sorry to have to call you, but your loan payment is three months overdue. We need to hear from you about getting this account caught up. Please call me."

Ben closed his eyes and leaned against the wall. Three months? He knew he'd been a little behind, but how had so much time gotten away from him? He also knew Lance had bent over backward to help with the loan due to their long friendship. He blew out a defeated breath.

"God, why? What am I supposed to do? I don't have the money." Despair enveloped him in a dark cocoon, and he just wanted to throw up his hands and walk away. He wouldn't have any income until the cattle were ready for market, which was still a few weeks away. He might have to sell some early, much as he disliked doing so. They wouldn't bring in nearly the price he needed.

Then a thought struck him. He did have something he could sell. Jolene's engagement ring. It had set him back a pretty penny, but it had been the one she wanted.

At least she'd had the decency to return it when she ditched him.

Rousing himself from his self-pity, he headed up the stairs to his bedroom and rummaged through the bottom drawer of his dresser until he found the small black box hidden under some old T-shirts. He really should have put the ring in a safer place, such as a safety deposit box at the bank, but at the time, he just wanted it out of his sight. It had sat there forgotten since the day Jolene handed it back to him.

He held the box in the palm of his hand, pushing the memories it evoked to the back of his mind where he wouldn't have to dwell on them. Finally, he flipped open the top, revealing the beautiful, one-carat, princess-cut diamond set in a white-gold band with smaller accent diamonds. As he gazed at the ring that had once graced Jolene's slender finger, he suddenly realized he felt nothing. The memories he had feared dredging up failed to make him sad. It was almost as though the past belonged to a completely different person, someone he had known a long time ago, but who had no connection to him today. Ben would have no problem parting with this ring. Besides, why keep it? It wasn't as if he had anyone else in mind to give it to. Even if there were, he wouldn't give another woman a second-hand engagement ring.

Now why had his thoughts roamed *there*? He snapped the lid closed and tucked the box into his shirt pocket. Tomorrow he would see what he could get for the ring and use the money to pay off some of the overdue loan. Depending on how much the ring might fetch, he might even be able to pay everything he owed. He realized he would have to sell the ring at a loss, but at least it would buy him some time. Then he could hold out until the cattle were ready to sell.

His immediate short-term problem worked out, he set about the many tasks he needed to get done.

CHAPTER FIVE

Ben was disappointed the following Sunday when Darcy didn't show up for their Sunday school class. A couple of the members asked about her, as though he should know her whereabouts, but he just shrugged. After all, he wasn't her keeper. He found his thoughts drifting, yet again, during the lesson. Had she not liked their church? Was she still looking around for a place where she fit in? He *had* invited her back when they'd talked at the clinic, and he'd thought she seemed receptive. Still, she hadn't actually said she would come back. Maybe he still made her uncomfortable. He mentally kicked himself.

He sat with Tim toward the front of the sanctuary during the worship service and forced his mind to focus on the Lord. As the service concluded, and people began filing out, he spotted Darcy in the last pew. She smiled when he caught her eye. Several people blocked the path between them, and Ben had to bide his time until people moved out of the way. He hoped she wouldn't leave before he was able to make his way to her. A few people tried to stop him to talk, but he waved them off, saying, "I'll catch you later."

Thankfully, Darcy didn't dart out immediately after

the service. She stood as though waiting for him.

"I'm sorry I'm late," she said when he reached her. "I had an emergency call this morning."

He found his muscles relaxing when he realized her reason for not being there earlier had nothing to do with him.

"Darcy!" cried Molly, parting the crowd like Moses parted the Red Sea to greet her. "We missed you this morning. I'm so glad you're here."

Darcy explained again about the delay.

"You're going to lunch with us?" Although phrased as a question, Molly's words came out more like an order.

Darcy hesitated, looking at Ben. He knew she was thinking about whether or not her presence would preclude him from going again.

"Please come," he said. "You can ride with me if you want."

Molly looked from one to the other and smirked. "Okay, you two. See you at Francine's." She scurried away and caught up to Tim.

"That's very nice of you," Darcy said. "By the way, how are your calves?"

"Oh, much better, thank you." He put his hand on the small of her back and steered her out into the foyer, where groups of people still lingered, then on to the parking lot. "That powder you gave me worked wonders."

She smiled. "I'm glad to hear it, but I don't think there's anything magical about the powder. I think it was your good nursing care."

"Regardless, I appreciate your help." He left his hand on her back, thinking how natural it felt, as they approached his truck. "I'm afraid my truck isn't as new or as nice as yours," he said, as he opened the passenger door. "Maybe I should have let you drive."

She laughed as she climbed into the seat, keeping her skirt tucked modestly around her legs. "We both drive working vehicles. Neither one of our trucks is for show."

Her remark stopped him for just a moment as a memory surfaced of Jolene wrinkling her nose at his truck. "Do we *have* to ride in this old thing?" she'd complained. "Why can't you buy something nicer?"

He closed the door, shaking his head, and trotted around to the driver's side. As he pulled out of the parking lot, his mind raced desperately for something to say.

"So, do you like living in Wyoming?" he finally asked.

She nodded, then replied, "Yes, for the most part, although I miss my family and friends back home in Pennsylvania."

He wanted to ask why she'd left but figured that was too personal, so he stayed silent.

"But I think what I miss most is riding my horse."

He shot her a sideways glance. "You have a horse?"

"Yes, but I didn't bring her with me because I didn't know whether I could find a place to stable her. I needed to get myself established first before moving her."

"And have you found a place to keep her?"

Darcy frowned. "I've looked at a couple of stables, but I was not overly impressed. I guess I'm spoiled by what I grew up with."

He looked at her again before turning his eyes back

to the road. "What do you mean?"

"My family owns a riding stable. We also board several horses and do a little breeding on the side. Our facilities have always been top-notch."

Ben's eyebrows shot up. So, this woman knew more about horses than he'd given her credit for. She probably knew way more than *he* did.

"Wow, I'm amazed. Why didn't you tell me?"

"You didn't ask." She seemed to wrestle with her answer for a minute before adding, "Not that I expect everyone to ask about my background. And I don't just tell my life's story to everyone I meet."

Not quite knowing how to process this revelation, Ben stayed quiet for a moment. Then, out of nowhere, he heard himself saying, "Well if you ever want to ride, you're welcome to use any of my horses."

She turned to him, her eyes wide. "Oh . . . I . . . well, thank you, but I couldn't take advantage."

For some reason, he found the idea of seeing her out at his ranch riding the horses pleasing. "It wouldn't be taking advantage, believe me. I've had to let some of my help go and, right now, I have more horses than people to ride them. They could use the exercise."

"Oh. I . . . don't know what to say."

"Say 'yes.' You'd be doing us all a favor." He peeked over at her, surprised to see a huge grin on her face.

"Yes!" She laughed. "Yes! Wow. I can't believe this."

He pulled into Francine's and found a parking spot. When he shut off the engine and went around to open her door, he noticed her wiping tears from under her eyes. Ben inadvertently extended his hand to help her down before realizing that she hopped in and out of a truck all day long.

"I don't know how to thank you, Mr. Parish," she said, as she accepted his hand.

"You can start by calling me Ben."

"Thank you, Ben." Tears still clung to her lashes as she smiled up at him.

"Shall we?" He motioned toward the restaurant. They walked in and found the rest of the group already seated. Knowing looks passed among the others as Ben and Darcy took the two open seats.

Although the group once again sat around a large table, the conversation tended to fracture into side discussions between two or three people. Ben found himself glad that Molly sat on the opposite side, unable to monopolize the talk between himself and Darcy, who he was finding more fascinating by the minute. When everyone else had finished and were getting up to leave, he realized he'd been so engrossed in talking to Darcy and excluding the rest of the group, that he had barely registered their presence. He didn't want to leave. And from the way in which Darcy remained in her seat as everyone else rose, he gathered that maybe she didn't want to go, either. They waved goodbye to the group, not missing Molly grinning at them as she trailed the rest to the door.

Darcy laughed. "Will we be a new hot topic of conjecture?"

Ben propped his elbow on the table and leaned toward her, his face in his palm. "Probably."

"Oh dear. I don't want to start rumors."

He shrugged. "People have to talk about something." He smiled at her drawn brow. "Look,

Darcy, I'm enjoying talking to you, that's all. If people want to read more into something that's not there, that's their problem."

She nodded. "I'm enjoying talking with you, too."

Just then, a thin, older woman with wispy graying-brown hair poking out of a hair net, wearing a stained red apron over jeans and a T-shirt, popped out of the kitchen and approached their table. Ben hopped up and pulled her into a tight hug. They seemed lost in their own little world for a moment before Ben released her and said, "Francine, this is my friend, Darcy Fuller. Darcy, this is *the* Francine."

Darcy started to rise, but the woman said, "No, don't get up." Instead, she pulled out a chair and plopped down next to Ben.

"It's nice to meet you, Francine," said Darcy. "The food here is wonderful."

"Thank you. We try. It's nice to meet you, too, Darcy." She asked a couple of casual polite questions before turning her attention back to Ben, her brows knitted in a frown. "Ben, I heard you sold Jolene's ring. Are you having financial problems?"

Ben felt the blood drain from his face. He loved Francine like a mother, but sometimes her frankness and her lack of discretion in airing his personal affairs in public made him cringe. He tried to plaster a smile on his face and reached for her dishwater-chapped hand. "Francine, there's nothing to worry about."

The woman's dark eyes searched his. "Ben, you know if you need anything—"

"I don't. Everything's fine." He pierced her with a stare, hoping to convey the message that he didn't want to talk about this subject in front of Darcy. Or ever, for that matter.

Apparently, Francine took the hint. "Okay, but you know I'm always here for you." She rose from her seat. "Gotta get back to work." She cast one more worried glance at him and disappeared through the swinging door into the kitchen.

Ben breathed out a sigh. It would be hard to pick up the thread of a pleasant conversation after Francine's ill-timed, embarrassing interruption. He knew Darcy had to be wondering what had just happened, but fortunately, she didn't ask.

"Well, I'd better get home and do some work," he said, pushing back his chair and standing.

"Yeah, me, too." Darcy didn't meet his eyes.

He reached for her ticket, but she placed her hand over it.

"No, you don't have to do that. I'll pay for my own." She extracted her wallet from her purse and headed to the cash register.

The ride back to the church became awkward again, with neither of them saying much. When they reached the parking lot, Darcy didn't wait for him to open her door.

She jumped out, then turned and said, "Thank you for everything. I had a great time. And if you meant what you said about riding your horses, could I take you up on it one afternoon this week?"

"Yes, of course. Just let me know when and I'll saddle one up for you." He found himself looking forward to seeing her again.

"Oh, no need. I can do that." She flashed him a sweet smile. "Thanks again." She closed the door and headed for her truck at the other end of the lot.

Ben waited until she had gotten in and started the engine before pulling out. Drat! Why had Francine picked that time when everything was going so well to have what should have been a private talk? Now things were strange between him and Darcy again.

CHAPTER SIX

Darcy checked the afternoon appointment schedule, delighted to see a familiar name. Molly Lewis had a two o'clock appointment, and even better, it was for a new puppy exam. Then, after appointments were finished, Darcy was heading out to Whispering Winds to take Ben up on his offer to let her ride one of his horses. She couldn't wait to be on a horse again. Things were definitely looking up.

A few minutes before two, Darcy heard Molly's voice in the waiting room, talking a mile a minute as usual. Not waiting for Pam to show her into an exam room, Darcy walked out into the lobby to greet her new friend and her new friend's adorable Golden Retriever puppy.

"I'm so happy you were able to see Della today," Molly said, as she accompanied Darcy back into the first exam room. "I just got her yesterday and I want to make sure she's healthy. I have two other dogs at home."

"She looks great," Darcy said, fondling the soft puppy fur while Della wiggled with delight. "But I'll check her over and do a stool exam for parasites."

Molly handed her the paperwork from the breeder, and Darcy studied it. "This looks like a good breeder. They've done everything they should have done before selling the puppy."

"They're the best. I got my two other dogs from them. I'm a Golden fiend."

Darcy folded the paperwork and handed it back to Molly. "Goldens are great dogs." She ran her hands over the puppy, examining her from head to tail. "Well, she looks healthy. The breeder gave her the first round of vaccines, so she's not due for another two weeks. I'll just get a stool sample, and then we'll be done."

Molly followed Darcy out to the lab area while she set up the sample. "So," Molly said, "it looks like you and Ben hit it off the other day. I guess he doesn't dislike you after all."

Darcy felt her cheeks growing warm and tried to busy herself with what she was doing.

Molly laughed. "Sorry, I didn't mean to embarrass you. But Ben's a great guy. He needs someone special in his life."

"Molly, we just met and we didn't get off to the best start. Don't make our friendship into something it's not." Maybe Darcy needed to turn the tables. "Besides, don't you have your eye on him?"

The other woman placed a hand on Darcy's arm. "Darcy, don't get me wrong. Ben is a wonderful man. And his looks would make any woman take notice. But there's never been anything between Ben and me. We are way too different. He's too quiet and I talk all the time, in case you haven't noticed."

"But that red-headed woman—shoot, I can't ever remember her name—indicated . . ." Darcy didn't really know what. It had just been something casual mentioned the first week they'd gone to lunch without Ben.

"Kendra?" Molly rolled her eyes. "She likes to constantly remind me about how I drooled over Ben when he first started coming to our church. Of course, that was before the whole Jolene fiasco. It's been over three years, and Kendra still won't let it go."

Darcy motioned for Molly to step back into the exam room while they waited for the test. After closing the door, she said, "Molly, can I ask you something that's none of my business? You can tell me if I'm out of bounds."

Molly put Della on the floor to explore while she settled back in her seat. "Fire away."

Darcy hesitated as she watched the curious puppy sniff everything in the room. She reached into the treat jar and handed Della a biscuit, which the puppy accepted with enthusiasm. Maybe Darcy shouldn't even bring the subject up. After all, Ben's personal life didn't concern her. So why did she want to know?

"What happened with Jolene?" she blurted out. Della stood on her rear legs, pawing at her for another treat. Darcy gently pushed the puppy's front feet off her legs.

Molly blew out a puff of air and rolled her eyes again. "Jolene. How Ben ever got hooked up with that piece of work I'll never know." She snapped her fingers for Della to come. The puppy bounded over to Molly, wagging her tail. Molly scooped her up into her arms. "It won't be long before I won't be able to do this with you, will it?" She snuggled against the puppy, then returned her attention to Darcy.

"Jolene just kind of appeared from out of nowhere, supposedly to help out with an elderly relative, Maudie Perkins. Her great-aunt, I think. Nobody knew a thing about Jolene, and she didn't share much about herself. Personally, I don't think her great-aunt needed help at all. Maudie gets along just fine and has more energy than most people half her age. I believe Jolene was running away from something and used Maudie as an excuse."

Darcy stepped around the exam table and sat on the bench next to Molly. She reached out to stroke the puppy, who now lay sound asleep in Molly's arms. "A tired puppy is a good puppy."

Molly smiled. "She goes full steam ahead and then crashes."

"So where did Ben meet Jolene?"

"I'm not entirely sure, but I think Ben went out to Maudie's house to deliver something from town. He's really sweet that way—dropping off supplies to elderly people whenever he has to go into town. Not that Maudie isn't perfectly capable of driving into town herself, but Ben saves people the trip whenever he can."

Darcy nodded. This was a side of Ben she hadn't known about. There were a lot of sides to Ben she didn't know about, although why it mattered so much to her, she couldn't say.

"Of course, that was before his dad died and his brother left and Ben had to take on the whole ranch by himself. But I know he still drops things off for people from time to time."

"So how did they end up together?"

"Well, I don't know how the relationship got started, but I can just picture him mentioning that he lived at Whispering Winds Ranch and her batting her sweet baby blues at him and saying, 'Ooh! You own a ranch? I would love to see it sometime.'"

"Jolene's pretty?" For some reason, Darcy dreaded the answer she knew was coming.

Molly wrinkled her nose. "Only on the outside."

"What do you mean?"

"Well, if you like a petite, blonde-haired, blue-eyed woman with a peaches-and-cream complexion and a fashion-model figure—and what man doesn't—then, yes, she's pretty. Stunning. Perfect, in fact." Molly huffed out a breath. "I'll bet she's left many broken hearts in her wake. But you know the old saying, 'beauty is only skin deep?'"

Darcy nodded.

"But ugly is to the bone."

Darcy raised her eyebrows.

"She reminded me of the time when Jesus called the Pharisees white-washed tombs. Beautiful on the outside but full of rotting bones on the inside."

"So how did Ben ever let himself become involved with a woman like that?"

Molly tightened her lips and shifted the sleeping puppy to her other arm. Della's amber eyes fluttered open briefly, then closed again. "I think she swept him off his feet. I mean, here is this beautiful woman suddenly hanging all over him and showing interest in everything about him. If she was doing anything to help Maudie, I don't know when, because she was constantly at the ranch or wherever Ben was. The next thing we knew, she had this gigantic engagement ring on her finger. The thing must have cost a small fortune."

"Did she come to church with Ben?"

"For a while. She came in the beginning, I think, to lay stake to her claim, then to show off her 'rock.' After that, there seemed to be one excuse after another. She had a headache or she was up late the night before or Maudie needed her to do something. As if. Maudie never misses a Sunday at the First Baptist Church on Main Street."

Darcy picked at stray hairs on her white lab coat. Her conscience needled her with little pricks of guilt for listening to the details of Ben's failed relationship, but she couldn't bring herself to stop. For some reason, it seemed important that she know what happened.

"We tried to warn him," Molly continued. "We could all see the woman was only interested in Ben because she thought he had money. He lived on this big ranch and, from all outward appearances, the family seemed well-to-do. She aimed to be a trophy wife for a rich man. I mean, look at the engagement ring. Ben would have never picked out anything so ostentatious. If he had picked it out, it would have been small and simple."

"What did he say when you tried to warn him?" Darcy now fiddled with the contents of her pockets.

Molly huffed out a brittle laugh. "Let's just say our good intentions were not well received. She had him wrapped around her little finger, and he was too blind to see it."

Darcy heard Pam bringing her next appointment back into the adjacent exam room. Maybe that was good, as it would end this gossip-fest. But she had to know one more thing. "So, what happened to break them up?"

Molly's eyes bore into hers. "What do you think? Money. Jolene found out Ben didn't have any money. When his dad died, and the financial status of the ranch came to light, she called it quits and high-tailed it out of here."

"She left town?"

"Yep. Nobody's seen her since. And Maudie seems to be doing just fine without her."

"Did Ben take it hard?"

Molly pondered for a moment. "I think he was secretly relieved."

Darcy stood. "Thank you for telling me. I won't say anything to Ben about what you told me."

Molly rose, as well, rousing Della. Molly put the puppy on the floor and attached the leash to her harness. "Does this mean you'll be talking to Ben sometime in the near future?" The edges of her lips twitched in a teasing grin.

Don't blush again. But her admonition didn't help, as the tell-tale heat suffused Darcy's face. "Yes. He invited me out to the ranch to go horseback riding."

"Horseback riding, huh?"

Darcy stammered. "Not together. It's not a date. He just said I could come out and ride his horses, you know, to exercise them. Because I miss riding my horse."

"Uh-huh." A full-fledged smile spread across Molly's face. "I understand."

"Molly, it's not like that." Darcy stopped. Her friend was clearly not buying the explanation. "Don't forget to make an appointment for two weeks."

"Oh, I won't." Molly opened the door to leave, waving over her shoulder. Della balked at her leash, forcing Molly to reach down and pick her up. Molly exited with a laugh. "Have fun with Ben."

CHAPTER SEVEN

Ben found himself impatiently awaiting Darcy's arrival, his Australian shepherd, Mack, apparently picking up on his tension. Mack had plastered himself next to Ben's side, hardly letting him move. Darcy had called earlier to say she'd be by around four-thirty if that was okay. Although she'd told him not to bother saddling up a horse, he'd gone ahead and done so. Malachi, a handsome, sorrel Quarter horse gelding, stood eager and ready to go in the paddock.

Ben had told Darcy the truth about the horses not getting enough exercise what with his having to lay off some of the ranch hands. Although it would have only made sense to sell a few of the horses, he couldn't bring himself to part with them. He had a history with most of the animals. Besides, he hoped the financial difficulty was only a temporary setback and he would soon be up and running at full capacity again.

He wished he could join Darcy for a leisurely ride, but he had way too much work to do. He always had way too much work to do. But—his spirits lifted—he could spare a few minutes to show her around. That would only be the polite thing to do. Yes, riding with her would be a good idea. Ben jogged back to the barn to saddle up Windsong, another Quarter horse, a beautiful red roan with a flaxen mane and tail. By the time he led her out into the paddock, he heard the sound of Darcy's Ford Ranger crunching up the long gravel driveway. She was going a bit too fast—spewing pebbles, with dust swirling around the vehicle. She must be impatient to ride. Mack barked and ran out to greet the visitor.

Ben waved and walked toward her as she stopped the truck and hopped out, a huge grin on her face.

"I'm so excited!" she greeted. "It's been way too long since I've been on a horse." She squatted down and gave Mack a thorough petting.

"Hello to you, too," Ben said, laughing, as he reached the truck and looked her over. She wore tight-fitting jeans tucked into riding boots and a beige sweater, with her thick hair pulled back in its usual ponytail.

She shot him a sheepish smile. "Sorry. I've been looking forward to this all day."

"Me, too." As the words left his mouth, he realized how dopey they made him sound, like he was a junior-high kid just counting the hours until he could see his crush. He needed to remember he had extended the invitation to her out of a desire to satisfy a need on both their parts—to exercise the horses and to do her a favor by allowing her to ride them. It wasn't as if he'd just been sitting around doing nothing, waiting for her to show up and make his day complete. He'd been busy. But, if he were honest with himself, he had to admit he had also harbored a certain degree of joyful anticipation for the afternoon.

Fortunately, she didn't seem to notice his

embarrassment, her attention still focused on Mack. "And who is this happy fellow?"

"That's Mack, cattle dog extraordinaire. He only has one bad habit. He thinks everyone has nothing better to do all day than pet him."

She gave the dog one last rub and straightened up. "Sorry to disappoint you, Mack, but I've got other plans." She started walking toward the paddock, Mack at her heels. "Oh, what beautiful horses." Malachi came over to investigate the visitor, and Darcy stopped at the rail, running her hand along his muzzle.

"This is Malachi, and the roan behind him is Windsong."

"Malachi and Windsong. What lovely names." She turned back to him. "Are there stories behind the names?"

Ben smiled. "Yes. Malachi means 'messenger of God.' He was born around the time my mom died. We kind of felt like God was sending us an angel to help us get through the grief." His voice took on a husky tone, and he coughed once, clearing his throat.

"I'm so sorry. That must have been a difficult time for you. I take it Malachi was born here at the ranch."

"Yes, all the horses we have now were born here. That's why . . ." He left the sentence unfinished. *That's why I can't bring myself to sell any of them.*

She didn't push. "What a timely blessing. And Windsong?"

Ben pulled his composure back under tight rein. "Well, of course, Windsong goes with the name of the ranch, Whispering Winds. But that's not really how she got her name. She was born during a ghastly storm. The timing seemed like it couldn't have been worse. But we wanted to remember the good that came out of that dreadful night."

"I like the name Windsong. Much better than Stormy."

"Yeah, we wanted something kind and gentle. My brother, Dave, wanted to name her Tornado."

Darcy rubbed Windsong's neck, fingering her tawny mane. "Tornado would never do for this delicate beauty."

"No, can't say that name would fit her personality. Oh, I almost forgot. I want to show you Star."

Darcy's eyes lit up. "The new foal?"

"She's not so new anymore. She's almost a month old." He walked toward the end of the barn where a lovely mahogany bay mare stood in the outside stall taking in the activity in the paddock. Ben stopped and scratched her chin. "This is Maggie. Star is in the back."

Darcy patted the mare's extended neck, then craned her own neck to see into the stall. "Oh! There she is!" Her voice rose in excitement, although she kept her volume soft. "I see the star on her head. What a gorgeous baby."

"She's doing well. Almost doubled her birth weight. Maggie's a good mother."

Darcy placed her hands on the door of the stall and leaned in closer. "I could stay here all day admiring them."

Ben laughed. "You're welcome to do so, but I thought you wanted to ride."

She turned to him and smiled. "Only the temptation to get on a horse could drag me away from looking at a precious foal."

He started walking back toward the paddock. "Then come on. Take your pick. We'll head out."

"Oh." Darcy seemed to suddenly realize he would be riding with her.

"Unless you prefer to ride by yourself."

"Oh, no, not at all. I just thought you might be too busy. But I told you not to bother saddling a horse for me."

"It's no problem." His mind reflected on Jolene. How he wished it would stop! Jolene had seemed perfectly happy to be at the ranch as long as she didn't actually have to *do* anything. She was scared of the cattle and the horses, and the few times he managed to get her in the saddle, she'd been nervous and uneasy. And as for her saddling up her own horse, that never would have happened.

Darcy smiled again, and it hit him how much he liked her smile. It was sweet and genuine, not at all like that fake smile Jolene planted on her face. Jolene again! He compressed his lips. Why did he keep comparing her to Darcy? It wasn't as though he had a romantic interest in Darcy. As pretty and nice as she was, he did not have any intention of going down *that* road again. Ever. He would keep her at arm's length just like all the other women since Jolene. Besides, she was interested in the horses, not him.

He shoved the unwelcome thoughts aside and opened the gate. "Why don't you take Windsong?" he suggested. "I have a feeling the two of you will get along fine."

"Okay."

Before he could move to help her into the saddle, she had the reins in her hand and her left boot in the stirrup. She swung her right leg up easily and settled into the saddle.

Stupid, she probably rides better than you do. She doesn't need a man to help her mount a horse. He climbed into his saddle and said, "I thought I could show you around the ranch a little if you'd like."

Her eyes shone. "I would like that. Thank you."

They took off at a slow pace, but it was obvious the horses were anxious to let loose. "It looks like these two aren't overly happy about a leisurely stroll. What do you say we race to the ridge up there?" He pointed to a sharply sloping area off in the distance. "That's where I graze most of the cattle."

She grinned. "You're on." She kicked her heels into Windsong's flanks and soon left him behind.

He chuckled and spurred Malachi into action. They crested the ridge to find Darcy waiting.

"What took you so long?" she said, her eyes twinkling with laughter.

"I gave you the faster horse."

"Uh-huh." She lifted her hand to her brow to block the sun. "Oh, Ben, it's beautiful up here."

Lush green meadows dotted with black cattle spread out as far as the eye could see.

"What magnificent animals. How many head of cattle do you have?"

"About seventy-five. At one time, we had several hundred. But the herd dwindled quite a bit after Mom died and Dad kind of lost interest in everything." He nudged Malachi into a walk and Darcy fell in beside him. "Then Dad died and my brother left and . . . well, it's been a little tough since then."

"I'm sorry. It must be hard having to do everything

by yourself."

He glanced over to see her look of compassion and didn't know quite how he felt about it. Ben was used to people sympathizing with him over the multiple misfortunes that had befallen his family since Mom's death, but he couldn't bear pity. And he didn't like burdening people with his troubles or talking about himself. Normally a private, quiet man who kept his worries to himself, Ben found himself wanting to open up and share more with Darcy. He didn't know why, exactly, but his instincts told him she would understand and empathize, yet not feel sorry for him.

"I don't do everything by myself. I have several ranch hands." He took off his hat and wiped the sweat from his brow with the back of his shirt sleeve. "We lost a number of cattle in a couple of storms . . ." Despite letting her have a tiny peek into his closed heart, there were some things he would not discuss, namely his financial struggles or Jolene. "But I'm slowly trying to build the herd back up."

They were approaching a cluster of grazing cattle who raised their broad heads and eyed the visitors with mild curiosity.

Darcy stopped well away from the group. "Are they docile?"

Ben replaced his hat and nodded. "For the most part, as far as beef cattle go. I don't keep any bulls, but there are several cows with calves right now, and they can be aggressive if they feel their babies are threatened."

"That's natural." Darcy looked off into the distance where two other men on horseback approached.

"Those are a couple of my guys, Cam and Ricky.

They're making the rounds. Come on, I'll introduce you." He trotted ahead of her toward the two ranch hands.

Darcy hung back a little as they talked, then moved slowly forward.

"Guys, I want you to meet Darcy Fuller. *Dr.* Darcy Fuller." Ben swept his arm toward her. "She's Doc Tippins' new associate vet. You'll probably be seeing a lot more of her around here."

Both men tipped their hats and said, "Ma'am," before turning their attention back to Ben, their raised eyebrows asking the unasked question.

"Nothing's wrong. The doc is just getting the lay of the land and enjoying a ride. Darcy's quite an experienced horsewoman, as well as a vet."

The two exchanged sly grins as burning crept up Ben's neck into his face. He would set them straight later. Narrowing his eyes at them and flashing what he hoped were warnings, he said, "Keep an eye on those three cows that are due to calve and let me know if there are any problems."

"Yes, boss," said Cam, his lips twitching in amusement.

As if they wouldn't. But he'd had to say something to disengage their imaginations. He turned to Darcy. "Shall we?"

She nodded. "It was nice meeting you," she called over her shoulder to the two men who stood looking on with amusement on their faces. When they were out of earshot, she said, "What was that all about?"

Ben feigned innocence. "What?"

"They seemed to find my presence humorous."

He sighed. "It's not you. It's me. I don't often ride

with a pretty woman by my side." Drat! Did he just say *pretty woman*? "I mean—"

"I think I know what you mean." Her eyes sparkling, she said, "Come on, show me the rest of the ranch."

CHAPTER EIGHT

Darcy couldn't believe how wonderful it felt to be on a horse again. She hadn't expected Ben to join her, but she was glad he did. Although she had a good sense of direction and didn't think she'd get lost, the ranch spread out over quite a few acres. Still, she'd bet money Windsong could find the way back home easily enough. But Darcy found she enjoyed Ben's company, and she was pleased he'd shared a bit of his personal life with her.

She hadn't let on that she knew far more about him than he had revealed to her. He hadn't said anything about his money problems, which was probably normal. Most people didn't like for others to know sensitive information like financial woes. But she couldn't help reflecting on how unfairly life had treated him. From everything she'd seen so far, Ben was a hard, honest worker who loved the ranch. He shouldn't have to struggle because of unfortunate circumstances beyond his control.

The sun had begun its descent toward the horizon, painting the sky in glorious shades of pink, amber, and purple, when they returned to the paddock. Ben dismounted and started to untack Malachi. Darcy followed suit with Windsong.

"You don't have to—"

"Of course, I do. I couldn't possibly leave you to put everything away after you were so kind to take the time to show me around." She flipped the reins over Windsong's neck and removed the bridle. "I appreciate you letting me ride."

Ben unbuckled the girth and replied, "My pleasure. You're welcome anytime."

"I will definitely take you up on that offer."

He removed the saddle and stood with it in his hands. "Do you have to get back right away?"

Darcy stopped and considered her answer. She wasn't on call tonight and had nothing pressing back at the clinic. "No, I guess not."

He motioned for her to follow him with the tack into the barn. Flipping on the light, he walked to a large room in the middle of the barn. Darcy closed her eyes for just a moment and took in the scent of leather and the earthy smells of horses and hay, immersing herself in the comforting odors that filled her with a sense of peace and belonging.

Ben poked his head out of the tack room door. "Darcy? Everything okay?"

Her eyes popped open. "Yes, sorry. I'm coming." She scurried after him. "I lost myself in the lovely aromas of the barn."

He laughed. "I'm not sure I've ever heard anyone describe how a barn smells in quite that way before."

"To me, it's a walk through the roses." She handed him the saddle and watched as he carefully wiped it down.

With his back still to her, he said, "I was thinking.

It's past dinner time. I have a couple of steaks in the refrigerator that need to be grilled." He turned and caught her eye for just a second before returning to his task. "There's plenty if you'd like to stay."

She mulled the proposition over in her mind. *Did she want to stay?* Yes, she did, and her pulse kicked up a notch at the thought. Then she chided herself. It was just dinner. Not a date. After what Ben had been through with his ex-fiancé, he had probably sworn off women altogether. Still, he *had* said Darcy was pretty and then became flustered. But she couldn't go down the whole relationship road either, not after Josh. She urged her silly heart to stop thudding so hard.

"I'd love to stay if you're sure it's okay."

He rubbed his hands on a cloth, hung it on a hook, and grinned. "Good. Come on." He flipped off the light switch in the tack room and led the way out of the barn. Dusk had settled, bringing tranquility to the landscape as they walked across the yard toward the large ranch house.

"My grandfather built this house back in the thirties. Of course, it's been remodeled and upgraded since then, but the basic structure is still the same." Ben took big strides with his long legs, forcing Darcy to sprint to keep up with him. He stopped and said, "Sorry. I'm used to walking fast. It seems like I always need to get somewhere in a hurry."

"It's all right. I do the same thing."

He slowed his pace and continued. "The house is way too big for just me, but when we had three generations living under one roof, it didn't seem big at all."

"Why didn't your brother stay?"

The light flicked off in Ben's eyes, as they seemed to gaze off into another place. "Dave never was a rancher. But despite knowing Dave didn't have ranching in his blood, I'd always harbored a secret hope that we would run the ranch together as our family has always done, but . . ." He stopped and a sad smile touched his lips as his eyes turned back to Darcy. "Dave hung on for Dad's sake, but when Dad died, Dave wanted to move on."

"What does he do now?"

They paused just outside the back door, where Ben carefully wiped his boots on a mat. Darcy wiped hers, as well.

"He's an architect in Denver. He wanted to escape the small town, rural atmosphere." Ben hit a switch that lit up the back patio and uncovered a propane grill. "I'm hoping to get him up here to help with some repairs to the house, but he stays busy."

Ben opened the screen door, which protested with a loud squeak, and preceded Darcy into the kitchen, where he turned on the lights.

Darcy stepped into the kitchen and looked around. "Wow. Your kitchen is huge. I could fit my whole apartment in here." She watched Ben rummage around in the refrigerator, finally pulling out steaks marinating in a plastic container, and a head of lettuce.

"Where do you live?" he asked, setting the food on a wooden kitchen island and going back for more.

"Near the clinic in those small apartment complexes off Main Street."

He set down carrots, a cucumber, and a tomato. "Here, you can put together a salad." He grabbed a knife from a knife stand near the sink. "Are you planning to stay there?"

She reached for the lettuce and took it to the sink, rinsing it under the faucet. "If I end up staying here, I'll eventually look for a house. Preferably somewhere with some land so I can have my horse."

Ben stopped what he was doing and looked at her, his eyebrows raised. "*If* you stay?"

Darcy shrugged. "I haven't made up my mind yet."

He remained quiet for a moment, then said, "I hope you do. I mean, Doc Tippins really needs the help."

She suppressed a grin. "May I have a bowl?" She reached for a paper towel from a dispenser next to the sink and patted the lettuce dry.

"What? Oh, yeah." He opened a cabinet and handed her a clear glass bowl. "You do like it here, don't you?"

"Yes. Very much." She tore lettuce into the bowl and reached for the carrots. "Do you have a vegetable scraper?" She became aware that he was just standing there, staring at her with those captivating blue eyes. "What's wrong?"

He shook his head. "Nothing." Pulling out a drawer next to the refrigerator, he produced a vegetable scraper and handed it to her.

His warm hand brushed hers, sending a shiver up Darcy's arm. Without meaning to, she raised her eyes to his, and heat rushed into her face. With a great effort, she tore her eyes away from his and took a step back.

Ben cleared his throat and said, "I'll go start the grill."

Darcy nodded, unnerved by the sensations coming over her. Taking a shaky breath, she forced herself to concentrate on preparing the salad. Fortunately, by the time Ben returned to put the steaks on the grill, she had managed to regain her composure.

They ate in a companionable silence interspersed with small talk. Toward the end of the meal, the conversation returned to her love of horses and the life she had left behind.

"It may be none of my business, but I'm wondering why you left Pennsylvania. You were obviously happy there."

Darcy sighed. Was she really ready to share her reasons? On one hand, she felt comfortable around Ben and instinctively knew he would understand. Besides, she knew a lot about his past, although the information had come from Molly, not him. Maybe if she shared more of herself with him, he would share more of himself with her. But they were just friends. There was no need to bare their souls to each other, right? And she had come here to make a fresh start and put everything behind her. She didn't want to drag her ugly baggage with her.

"I'm sorry, I shouldn't have brought it up." He reached across the table and laid his hand over hers.

She bit her lip. Darcy knew if she allowed herself to talk about her past, the tears would inevitably follow, and she didn't to cry in front of this man who she barely knew but was beginning to like quite a bit. A lot of men were uncomfortable around weeping women. Right now, she wanted to maintain some degree of self-control.

"Maybe we can talk about it another time. I don't want to spoil this lovely evening."

He withdrew his hand and smiled. "Of course."

Ben had inadvertently caused her to remember how happy she had been at her parents' stable, giving riding lessons, trail rides—wait! An idea popped into her head.

Her eyes widened and her voice rose in excitement. "Ben, I have an idea."

He looked momentarily taken aback by this abrupt change in her demeanor. Chuckling softly, he said, "Okay. What is it?"

Darcy fidgeted in her seat, as her words spilled out. "You said the horses need exercise."

"Yes—"

"And I love to ride."

"Yes, and I said—"

"What would you think about me giving trail rides on your ranch?"

"Trail rides?" His eyes narrowed in confusion.

"Yes!" She hopped up and paced the length of the large kitchen, her hands punctuating the air with her words. "We're not that far from Jackson Hole, where a lot of tourists visit. Tourists love trail rides. It would be a way to exercise the horses, make some money, and let me do something I love."

"But—"

"Tourists would probably get a kick out of seeing a working ranch. And we could think about sleigh rides in the winter, even consider riding lessons."

Ben ran his hand through his hair and took a deep breath. "Wow, I don't know, Darcy."

She plopped back down in her chair and, in her excitement, grabbed his arm. "Ben, just think about it. This could be an awesome opportunity for both of us."

He shook his head. "I don't have time to manage anything else."

"I'll do it. You wouldn't have to do anything. I have

the experience and the—"

"But what about your job?"

She withdrew her hand and lowered her eyes. "The truth is, I'm not all that busy."

"You're still getting established. You'll be busier."

Darcy looked up, her eyes fixed on his. "If that happens, we can hire help. I know what I'm doing. It's what I've done my whole life."

She could see the wheels turning in his mind. This venture could help the ranch financially, not that Darcy had blurted out her idea with money being her primary motivation.

He rubbed his chin between his thumb and forefinger and nodded. "It might work. It just might." He fixed his eyes on her. "Providing you stay."

She felt a smile stretching across her face.

Darcy drove home that night in a state of exhilaration. Not only had she had a wonderful time with Ben, but the proposition of a side business from which they could both benefit stirred her with renewed passion. Her thoughts chased each other around in her head as she considered all the work she needed to do to get this project up and running. The ringing of her cell phone startled her out of her mental checklist.

She picked it up and glanced at the caller ID. Then her heart skipped a beat. Josh! After all this time? What could he possibly have to say to her? With a trembling hand, she swiped the call off, letting it go to voicemail. She drove until she could find a place to pull over. Holding the phone to her ear, she pressed play.

"Darcy? Hey, it's Josh." Her throat tightened at the sound of his voice. "Look, I really need to talk to you. Could you please call me back?" The call disconnected.

She sat holding the phone, her body chilled and shaking all over. Then she pushed delete and slid the phone back into her purse before pulling back out on the road.

CHAPTER NINE

"So, what do you think, Francine?" Ben sat across the table from Francine in her cozy kitchen as he outlined Darcy's idea.

The older woman mused for a moment before answering. Then a sweet smile began in the corners of her mouth and worked its way up to her eyes. "I think it's a good idea."

Ben felt his tense muscles relax. "You do? Really?"

Francine reached across and squeezed his hand. "Yes, I do. This could not only bring in some extra income, but it could put Whispering Winds on the map."

Ben's brows drew together across his forehead. "I'm not sure I ever gave much thought to putting Whispering Winds on the map. All I've ever wanted was to run my ranch."

"I understand, but you've been running the ranch at a loss since Justin died."

He let out a sigh, closed his eyes, and massaged his temples. "I feel like I've let everyone down. Dad, Grandpa . . ." His words trailed off.

"Ben Parish, that's pure nonsense and you know it," Francine said, a hint of scolding in her tone. She rose and retrieved the coffee pot from the counter. After refilling their cups, she went on. "You've been dealt a lousy hand to play, but you're doing the best you can. That's all anyone can ask."

Ben took another sip of his coffee. "Sometimes I feel like I'm sinking in quicksand."

"Look at me, Ben."

He raised his eyes and met her direct gaze.

"You know I love you like my own son. But I was disappointed you didn't confide in me when you started having troubles."

Ben sighed again. "I don't like burdening you with my problems. I don't like burdening *anyone* with my problems."

"I'm not just anybody, Ben."

He forced a smile. "I know, Francine, but there's nothing you could have done."

"I could have listened."

"You're listening now."

She nodded. "Okay, then, enough of my reprimanding. Let's talk about this new enterprise you're considering."

Ben felt a genuine smile lifting his cheeks. "I have to admit, at first, when Darcy suggested conducting trail rides at the ranch, I was dumbfounded. I mean, the thought of having strangers traipsing across my land made me apprehensive. You know what a private person I am."

She snorted. "Oh, don't I?"

"But the more I thought about it, the more the idea grew on me. And not just because I could use the extra income, although I do admit that's a bonus. I like the idea of seeing the ranch come alive again, even if it's not quite the way I envisioned."

Francine fixed him with a knowing look. "And I don't suppose seeing more of Darcy has anything to do with your decision."

Warmth flooded his face, and he looked away. "Darcy and I are just friends and, I guess, soon-to-be business partners."

"Uh-huh. Not buying it, Ben. I see how your eyes light up when you talk about her."

He rose and deposited his mug in the sink. With his back still toward her, he said, "Francine, don't make more of this relationship than is really there."

Francine got up and placed an arm across his back. "I know you've been badly burned in the past, but you can't let one bad experience keep you from opening your heart again."

Ben turned and pulled her into a hug. "Francine, trust me. I've got way too much going on in my life right now to think about getting involved with another woman. Besides, you're the only woman I want."

She smacked him playfully and looked up into his face. "Sometimes God puts the right people in our path, whether we're looking for them or not."

He kissed the top of her head. "Sorry, but you're wrong this time. Jolene closed that door for me."

Francine disengaged herself and stepped back. "Jolene," she sneered. "Everyone could tell she was nothing but a gold digger."

He barked out a mirthless laugh. "Everyone but me."

She reached for his hand and drew him back to his chair. Seating herself, once again, across the table, she said, "Sometimes we make mistakes, Ben. But we learn from our mistakes and move on."

"Exactly. I learned I would never let another woman do to me what Jolene did."

Francine pursed her lips. "That's not what I mean, and you know it. You can't let what happened with Jolene keep you locked away inside yourself, afraid to love again."

"Love?" His eyes widened. "Whoa, I barely know Darcy."

"You know enough. She's kind and smart and genuine. I've observed her at the restaurant. With all the people I deal with every day, I'm a pretty good judge of character."

He held out his palms. "Fine, I'll grant you that. But don't be planning a wedding, because no matter how kind and smart and genuine Darcy is, I'm not interested in becoming romantically involved with her or anyone else. Subject closed."

Francine blew a noisy breath out through her lips. "Whatever you say." Hopping up, she said, "I've got a restaurant to open and you've got a ranch to run, so get on home."

Ben got up and hugged her again. "Thanks, Francine. I love you."

"Love you, too." As he placed his hat on his head and turned to the door, she added, "Remember I'm always here for you. Don't keep me in the dark."

He laughed. "No, ma'am. Besides, in this little town, nobody stays in the dark very long."

As Ben drove back to the ranch, he reflected on his

heart-to-heart talk with Francine. It had been way too long since he had actually sat down and talked to her, and he regretted that. He knew she always looked out for his best interests. Why had it taken her confronting him about selling Jolene's ring for him to trust her with his dire financial situation? She would have done whatever she could to help. The thing was, he knew she couldn't afford to help him, and he wouldn't have taken her money even if she could. His pride would never allow that. He felt his jaw clenching in his pride, and he chuckled to himself. Still, a man had to have some self-respect.

His thoughts turned to Darcy. Thankfully, she didn't know about his money woes. Otherwise, he would never have taken her up on her suggestion of conducting trail rides. If he thought for a moment she had only volunteered because she felt sorry for him . . . well, that would never do. He would not take charity, especially from her. If they were going into business together, he had to be sure she respected him. And what woman could respect a man who couldn't make his own way in the world?

Certainly not Jolene. He guessed he couldn't blame her for not wanting to marry someone who was broke. A wife needed financial security from her husband. Shoot, Jolene needed a lot more than financial security. A roof over her head and food on the table would never be enough to satisfy a woman of her expensive appetites. Why hadn't he seen her for the blood-sucker she was? She'd expected to be the queen of the manor with servants to do her bidding while she passed away the hours in mindless activities.

He remembered Darcy's comment about how much

she liked the smell of the barn, contrasting her again to Jolene, who wrinkled her nose in repulsion every time she stepped near the place. She rarely ventured off the porch unless he insisted. His blindness to her true nature only made him more determined not to entangle himself in another disastrous relationship, despite what Francine said. He couldn't trust his own judgment. Darcy was wonderful, and he enjoyed the time he spent with her, but they couldn't take things any farther. Not that Darcy gave any indication she wanted to take things farther.

He sensed she'd been hurt badly, too, which is why she'd moved far away from home. He wished she trusted him enough to tell him what had happened but, then again, maybe they were better off keeping their relationship strictly professional. He didn't even want to imagine what could happen to their business arrangement if they became romantically involved and it didn't work out. No, he needed to take a step back. Inviting her to have dinner with him the other night had probably been a mistake. He didn't want to lead her on or give her the wrong impression. Still, the idea of seeing her regularly gave him a thrill he couldn't deny.

CHAPTER TEN

Darcy spent the next couple of weeks working to make the business a reality. After scoping out the competition in the surrounding area and determining there was room enough for one more riding stable, she applied for a stable license. Then she spent several hours on the computer researching the various insurance policies before making an appointment to talk with an agent. She called Ben to see if the accountant who handled the finances for Whispering Winds Ranch could set up a separate account for the new business, and finally, before setting up a bank account, she drove out to the ranch to discuss names for the business with Ben.

She really didn't have to drive all the way out to the ranch to choose a name for the business, but she needed to go over everything she had already done to bring him up to speed as to where they were. Besides, it was a good excuse to see Ben, although just why she needed an excuse to see him, she didn't know. After all, they were going to be business partners. Still, it had been several days since she'd seen him, and she found herself looking forward to their meeting.

Without trying to analyze the fluttering of her heart

at the anticipation of seeing him again, she rolled down her window and relished the fresh, sweet-smelling breeze that blew in, filling her with renewed hope. It had been a long time since Darcy had been this excited about anything. If the past few months had been any indication of the way the rest of her life would go, she hadn't expected to feel anything, period. All she had wanted to do was exist, getting through one day at a time.

As she pulled up to the house, Ben came out the back door wearing a big smile. Mack followed, barking out a greeting.

"Good morning," Ben called out. His long legs crossed the short distance in a few easy strides, despite Mack running in circles around his feet. He reached the truck, where she sat gathering several folders from the passenger seat. "Here, let me take those."

She handed him the folders through the open window. Before she could get out of the truck, he had opened the door for her. Darcy couldn't help the grin creeping across her face. Ben was such a gentleman. She wasn't used to having doors opened for her.

Before she could say anything, he pulled her into a quick side hug. "It's good to see you." He released her and said, "Come in out of this hot sun and show me what you've brought. I made some lemonade."

"Sounds wonderful." She stooped down to give Mack a quick pat, then matched her steps to Ben's long strides and waited for him to open the creaky screen door.

"I need to get some WD-40 on that thing." He laughed. "Someday."

Darcy entered the cool kitchen, where a ceiling fan

stirred the sluggish air, and took the seat she had occupied when they'd had dinner a couple of weeks before. Ben laid the folders in the center of the table, then turned to the cabinet next to the sink and removed two glasses.

"It looks like you've been busy," he said, as he filled the glasses with ice and poured the lemonade. He set the two glasses on the table and took the seat across from her.

"I have." She took a sip of the lemonade. "Wow, this is really good."

"Thanks. It's a secret family recipe."

Her eyebrows shot up in surprise. "You made this from scratch?"

He chuckled. "No, not really. It's store-bought. That's our family secret."

She laughed with him, catching the merriment in his eyes as he gazed at her.

"Okay, down to serious business." He picked up the first folder, looking over the application for the business license.

She reached over and pointed to the document. "They're still processing the application, then they will have to come out and do an inspection."

He nodded. "Shouldn't be a problem."

"No, you have a beautifully maintained stable."

"Thank you." He closed the folder and moved it to the side. "What's next?"

"Insurance."

"Ah, the necessary evil." He fingered through several pages in the second folder.

"You can look over what I've done, but after researching the different companies and our needs, I think we should go with Equine Experts, the one on the top. They strictly insure horses and equine facilities. I have an appointment tomorrow to talk with one of their agents. That is if it's all right with you."

"Sounds good." He took a long gulp of his lemonade and got up to refill his glass. "More lemonade?"

"No, thank you. You can go with me if you want."

"I'd like to, but I have some other business to take care of. Besides, I trust your judgment." He settled back in his chair and grinned at her.

Warmth surged through her at his declaration of trust. How different from their first meeting. "Okay, I'll take care of it. But you can read over the information I downloaded from their website. Speaking of which, we will need to get a website."

"Tim, at church, does website design. We can ask him." Ben set the second folder aside.

"He does? That's perfect!" She couldn't believe how easily everything seemed to be falling into place. "Now, before we open a business bank account and register as a legal entity, we need a name for the business. By the way, I don't suppose you know a lawyer who can do the paperwork for us?"

He shook his head. "Sorry. But the insurance agent can probably recommend someone."

She pulled a notebook from the third folder and wrote herself a note to ask. "What about a name?"

"Ben and Darcy's?"

"Are you serious? It sounds like an ice cream company."

He chuckled. "Yeah, I guess it does. Look, it shouldn't be complicated. The ranch already has a name. Just call the business Whispering Winds Riding Stable."

She mulled his suggestion over. It made a lot of sense to keep things simple rather than having two different names for the same facility. "That's fine with me. Whispering Winds, it is. Anyway, I love the name. I suppose there's a story behind the ranch's name, also?"

His eyes shone with a love for his home. "When the wind blows through the trees, it makes the most beautiful whooshing sound. Almost like a prayer."

"Except, I'm guessing when there's a tornado."

He grinned. "Yes, during bad storms, the wind sounds more like the devil on a rampage." He sighed. "Okay, how are we going to book the rides? I don't want to put in a new phone system."

"We can do all that online. That's how most of the other stables work."

"Sounds good. I suppose Tim can handle that detail when he designs the website." He frowned. "I don't know what he charges, but I'm sure he'll give us a good price. By the way, how are we financing the startup costs?"

Darcy waved his question aside. "I've got it handled."

"What do you mean? I can't let you pay for everything out of your own pocket."

"I'll get the fees back once we start making money."

He stood and crossed over to the counter, laying his hands on the surface, his back toward her. "Darcy, no."

She rose and put a hand on his arm. "Ben, it's okay. Really. I'm keeping track of expenses on a spreadsheet until your accountant gets the business set up. Besides, this was my idea in the first place, so I should be the one to put up the initial costs."

He turned and faced her. "How much are we talking about?"

"A few hundred dollars. Not much."

He frowned. "Look, Darcy, I appreciate that this was your idea. But you're already doing most of the work. I can't let you—"

"I'll get the money back. You're providing the land, the horses, and the cost of caring for and feeding the horses."

His eyes hardened. "We haven't even discussed your fees. Or what to charge."

She sat back down, and he followed. "Honestly, Ben, I'd do it for free—" she held up a hand to prevent his protest—"because I love riding so much. But let me put some figures together, then we'll run them by the accountant. I suggest we start by charging less than what the other stables are charging, maybe offer discounts or specials until we start getting clients."

He nodded, and she was glad they had momentarily dropped the subject of the startup costs. She knew how financially strapped he was, and she had some money saved. The last thing she wanted was for Ben to go even further into debt for something that had the potential to go belly up. Not that she expected the business to fail, but sometimes things happened that were beyond people's control. This venture had been her idea. She should take the initial risk.

Picking up the last folder, Darcy called Ben's attention to a few other details before glancing at her watch. "I'm sorry, but I have to be back in the office for afternoon appointments." She finished her lemonade and stood to go.

He rose slowly, seeming to be in no hurry to see her leave. She studied him, unable to read the strange expression that had come over his face. Finally, he spoke, his voice husky. "Thanks, Darcy. For everything."

"Of course, partner." She picked up her folders and headed toward the door. "You don't need to see me out. I know the way."

"I want to."

They walked to her truck, his normally long strides considerably shorter. Then he took her hands in both of his and gazed at her for a long moment. "I think you and I will make a good team."

A smile tugged at her lips. "I think so, too." She extracted her hands, realizing she didn't want to let go, and climbed into her truck, feeling warm all over.

As she headed down the driveway, her phone rang. She picked it up and checked the caller ID. Oh no. Josh again. She had forgotten about his call a couple of weeks ago. A heaviness settled in her stomach. Dropping the phone to the seat, she ignored the call, debating on whether or not she would listen to his voice message, should he leave one. Why was he calling her? Curiosity and apathy warred with each other in her brain. She had left him behind. Or, rather, he had left *her*. But she was not going to allow him to worm his way into her heart again. He had already broken her heart beyond repair, leaving her with nothing left to give.

Darcy put the call out of her mind as she dealt with her afternoon appointments. For once, the schedule had been full and she remained busy. Only after she went home and picked up her phone to call her parents did she remember Josh's call. Should she listen to his message? She bit her lip, then, letting out a sigh, pushed play.

"Darcy, it's me again. Please call me. I need to talk to you."

"No, you don't, Josh. Besides, I have nothing to say to you. Please stay in the past where you belong." She deleted the message and called her parents.

"Darcy!" Her mother's excited voice blasted in Darcy's ear, forcing her to pull the phone away. "It's so good to hear from you. We miss you, honey. How are things going in Wyoming?"

Darcy filled her mother in on her and Ben's plans for the trail riding business. "I wanted to get your advice, Mom. What else should I be doing?"

She heard a palpable pause on the other end of the line. "I guess you're serious about staying out there." A hint of disappointment rang in her mother's tone.

"Yes, Mom, I am. I'm starting to fit in here and I'm really happy about the opportunity to start up a trail riding business. You know how much I loved working at our stable."

"I was hoping you'd reconsider and come home. We need you here, Darcy."

Darcy laughed. "Mom, you don't need me. You have lots of employees."

"Employees aren't family. Fuller Farms is a family business."

A sliver of regret pricked Darcy's heart. As an only child, naturally, her parents had expected her to take over the family business one day. She had let them down by moving to Wyoming.

"I know, Mom, but you know why I had to leave."

"Oh, Darcy, lots of people have disappointments in their life. But they don't just give up and run away."

She knew her mother viewed Wyoming as a temporary refuge in which to lick her wounds and heal before coming to her senses and returning home to where she belonged.

"There's something else you should know," her mother said.

"What?" Darcy's heart began to hammer against her ribs. Was one of her parents ill? Was there a problem with the stable?

She heard her mother's sigh. "Josh and Zoe broke up."

Darcy's heart climbed into her throat, rendering her unable to speak. Maybe that was why Josh had been calling her.

"Look, honey, I know you were hurt, but—"

Anger replaced the paralyzing numbness that had seized her at her mother's announcement. "Hurt? I was devastated, Mom. Humiliated."

"I know, honey, but people make mistakes."

Darcy blew out a long breath through her nose. "What are you trying to say, Mom?"

"I think you should at least talk to Josh."

Darcy rubbed the strip of skin between her eyebrows, willing herself not to get a tension headache. "I don't have anything to say to him."

"Darcy, Josh was the love of your life for more than three years. You can't just turn off your feelings like a faucet."

"He betrayed my trust. They both did. I can't just

forget that."

"Nobody is asking you to forget. But you can forgive."

"I've already forgiven them." Had she? Darcy really couldn't answer that question. But she wasn't going to analyze where she stood on forgiveness right now with her mother.

"You should give him another chance, honey."

"What? No!" Darcy stood and started pacing the length of her small living room. "I could never trust him again."

"Like I said, Darcy, people make mistakes. They deserve a second chance."

Darcy silently acknowledged her mother's words. "I don't deny that. But Josh's actions killed any love I had for him. There's nothing left."

"Love can be rekindled."

She closed her eyes, willing herself to remain calm. "I don't want to rekindle anything with Josh. I don't understand how you can defend him, Mom."

Her mother's voice softened. "Deep down, he's a good man, Darcy. A good man who greatly regrets what he did."

Darcy plopped back down on her sofa, hanging her legs off the end. "Mom, be honest. Do you think I should get back together with Josh because it's the right thing for both of us or do you just want me to come home?"

A long silence ensued. She finally said, "Both, I guess."

A humorless laugh escaped Darcy's lips. "Mom, I really can't think about Josh right now. I'm in the process of starting up a new business."

"That's another thing. What about this man you're going into partnership with?"

"Ben? What about him?"

Was it possible to hear someone pursing her lips over the phone? Or had Darcy just imagined her mother's pinched expression in her mind's eye? "You hardly know anything about him. Are you sure you're not just rebounding from Josh?"

"Of course not! Ben and I don't have romantic feelings for each other." Even as the words left her mouth, her lips curled up at the image of Ben. She tightened her lips and shook her head. "We're business partners, that's all."

"Darcy, you also have to be careful about who you go into business with."

"I know that, Mom. He's a good, trustworthy man."

"How can you possibly know after such a short time?"

"I just do, Mom."

Her mother huffed into the phone. "And what if things don't work out? You'll have invested a lot of money and time, as well as emotional involvement. In some ways, going into business with another person is almost like a marriage."

Darcy smiled at her mother's analogy. "I don't think there's anything to worry about. It's not like we're starting up a major corporation. It's just a simple side business."

"Nevertheless, get everything in writing and have a lawyer look it over before you sign anything."

Darcy rubbed her hand across her forehead. "I will. Mom, I need to go. I'll talk to you later."

"Pray about your decisions, honey. I love you."

"Love you, too, Mom. Bye." Darcy pressed the end call button before her head could explode.

She had thought her mother would be happy for her. Instead, she had cast doubt and offered one objection after another. Darcy sat wrapped in a cloud of gloom, trying to assimilate this new information about Josh.

How did she truly feel about Josh? She tried to search her heart for an honest answer but came up empty. Did he even want to get back together, or was that only wishful thinking on her mother's part? How did Darcy feel about going home? Her talk with her mother had added to her homesickness, which only confused her more. She was just beginning to get established here.

Suddenly, Ben's face popped into her mind. If she left now, it would be one more person who made promises and then walked out on him. Didn't she owe him something after talking him into the whole trail-riding idea? Of course, someone else could take the business over if he still wanted to move forward.

"God, what should I do?" she asked wearily.

No answer rumbled from heaven.

"Well, I prayed about it, Mom." She rose and went into the bathroom to get ready for bed.

CHAPTER ELEVEN

"Dave! Over here!" Ben shouted across the lobby of the crowded airport. His brother's face lit up as he made his way through the mass of people.

"Great to see you, little brother," Dave said, dropping his bags on the ground and pulling Ben into a bear hug.

"You too, man." Ben slapped his brother on the back and stepped back. They stood appraising each other for a long minute before Ben said, "Here, let me take one of those bags." He grabbed a heavy duffel bag and headed for the door. "How was your flight?"

"About as expected. But for an hour and a half, I can put with almost anything. Even a nonstop talking seatmate."

Ben winced. "Next time pretend you don't speak English." As they walked to the truck, he said, "It's been too long. You haven't been back since after Dad died."

"Yeah, I know. I meant to, but you know it is."

"I guess that means business is going well."

Dave laughed. "Too well. Some days I meet myself coming and going. But it pays the bills."

Ben nodded. "I'm glad you're here. I've got a lot of

work for you."

Dave contorted his face into a wry smile. "You do remember I'm not big on roping cattle."

"I remember. I promise, no cattle roping. But several repairs around the house need attention.

"You also remember I'm an architect, not a contractor?"

They reached the truck and Ben tossed the duffel bag into the back. "Yeah, seems I heard that somewhere. But hey, architect, contractor, whatever. I'm not picky as long as you help me with the house. There're a lot of projects that need to be done that I don't know how to do."

Dave hurled his bag into the truck bed. "I see you're still driving this old heap."

Ben shrugged. "At least until our rich uncle dies and leaves us a small fortune."

"That could be a long wait unless Gramps sowed some wild oats we don't know about." Dave opened the door and climbed in.

As Ben pulled out of the parking lot, Dave turned to him. "So seriously, Ben, how are things?"

Ben kept his eyes forward. "I'm doing okay."

"What's okay mean?"

Ben sighed. "I'm managing to keep my head above water. Once some of the steers are ready for auction, I should have a decent amount of money." He could feel his brother's burning eyes on him and felt the need to put a more positive spin on his situation. "Oh, and a partner and I are starting up a side business which should bring in some extra income." He risked a glance at Dave before returning his eyes to the road.

Dave narrowed his eyes. "What kind of side

business? You're not thinking about making moonshine, are you?"

Ben laughed, his tense muscles relaxing. "No. Nothing illegal." He proceeded to fill Dave in on Darcy's idea as they drove the several miles back to the ranch.

Dave sat for a long time without commenting. Then he said, "So you had to let some of the hands go?"

Ben swallowed and nodded, his chest starting to tighten again.

"Why don't you sell off some of the horses? They're a huge financial drain."

"I don't know," Ben answered truthfully. "I just can't. Sentimental reasons, I guess. They were all born at the ranch."

"That's not very practical, little bro. Yard ornaments cost a lot of money."

Ben turned into the long drive leading to the house. "I know. That's partly why I thought this trail-riding business would work. It'll bring in some extra cash and let me keep the horses at the same time."

Dave chewed on his lip but didn't reply. Mack ran out to greet them as they pulled up to the house. Dave threw open his door and allowed the excited dog to jump all over him. "Mack, buddy! You remember me!"

"Of course he does," Ben said, coming around to retrieve the bags. "Mack, get down." He pushed the dog off his brother. "His feet are all dirty. Look what he's done to your pants."

Dave glanced down at the muddy paw prints on his clean khakis. "Doesn't matter. They'll wash." He ruffled the thick fur behind Mack's ears. "What's a little dirt between friends?"

Mack danced around the brothers as they walked into the house. "You and your muddy feet stay outside," Ben said, closing the screen door behind them.

Dave set his bag down and looked around. "Everything looks the same. Just as I remembered it."

Ben raised his eyebrows.

Dave laughed. "That's a good thing, bro. Believe it or not, I've missed the old homestead."

"Yeah, well, as I said, there's a lot of work that needs to be done around the house, and not only have I been too busy to take care of a lot of things, but I don't have the expertise."

Dave rubbed his hands together. "Okay. Let me stash my bag in my old room and point me in the right direction."

The next morning, Ben and Dave worked side-by-side replacing rotten boards on the front porch.

"I'm sure glad we're getting this project done," Ben said around a mouthful of nails. "Even though everybody knows to come to the back door, I'd hate for some unsuspecting soul to fall through these old boards and break their leg."

Dave yanked up a rotten board and tossed it into a growing pile in the front yard, where it landed with a thud against several other boards. "With another few hours' work, it'll be good as new. Then we can move on to the upstairs plumbing." He chuckled. "Some vacation."

"Hey, don't complain. You have free room and

board." Ben looked up as the sound of a truck pulling into the driveway caught his attention. He stood, removed the nails from his mouth, and brushed the dirt off his hands. "As a matter of fact, you can take a break. Come meet Darcy."

They walked out to where Darcy had pulled the truck into the shade of a large live oak tree. Mack barked happily at the sight of the familiar truck.

"No jumping," Ben scolded, as Darcy got out, bearing an armful of folders and her laptop.

"I need to get a briefcase," she said. Then she caught sight of Dave. "Oh, hello."

"Darcy, I'd like you to meet my brother, Dave. Dave, Darcy Fuller."

"Nice to meet you," Dave said, extending his hand. He pulled it back abruptly and wiped it on his pants. "Sorry, I'm a bit grubby. We've been working on the porch all morning."

Darcy smiled. "No problem. It's nice to meet you, too, Dave. I've heard a lot about you."

"Don't believe whatever Ben told you. I'm the good brother."

"And I'm the good-looking brother," Ben quipped.

She laughed. "I'm not about to get in the middle of that argument." She shifted the contents of her arm into her other arm. "Have I come at a bad time? I don't want to interrupt your work."

Ben reached out and relieved her of her load. "Not at all. We needed a break."

"I should have called first, but I was just too excited. I've got all the paperwork ready to sign so we can get up and running."

"Come in and let's see what I'm signing my life

away for." Without thinking, Ben clutched the paperwork and her laptop in one arm and draped his other arm across her shoulder, leading her toward the house. In the few steps it took to reach the kitchen door, he realized how natural his arm felt over her shoulder. He dismissed the thought as they entered the house.

The coolness of the kitchen felt good compared to the blazing heat outside. Ben laid everything on the table, wiped his sleeve across his sweaty forehead, and pulled three water bottles from the refrigerator. He sank down across from Darcy and took a long swig of his water.

"I'll go back and work on the porch while you two talk," said Dave.

"No, stay." Ben patted the seat next to his. "You need a break and, besides, I want you to be in the loop. I value your input."

Dave cast a wary look at Darcy but did as Ben requested.

Darcy reached for the first folder. "These are all the legal documents. There's a copy for you to keep in the back of the folder. The paralegal marked every place that needs a signature."

Ben took the thick packet of papers and did a cursory look over it. "As if I can understand all this legal mumbo-jumbo."

While he perused the documents, she went on. "The inspection is scheduled for Friday if that works for you."

"Friday's fine. I'll have Dave up early to muck out the stalls." Ben shot a teasing glance at his brother.

"Ha, ha. No, thank you. I do not muck. I did enough of that growing up. The mucking is all yours, bro.

That's why I moved to the big city."

"You see what I have to put up with?" Ben got up to fetch a pen from the kitchen drawer. "Hopefully this one writes." He spent several minutes initialing and signing forms. "All done. What's next?"

"The bank." Darcy pulled out another folder with less papers. "And the insurance. I also have some paperwork from the accountant. Then, if you have time, I want to show you the website Tim set up."

"Did Tim get us a bill for the website?"

"All taken care of." Darcy averted her eyes and booted up her laptop.

Ben frowned. He had told Tim to give him the bill. "How much?"

"Not much, considering all the work he did." Darcy continued to fiddle with the computer.

Ben flattened his lips. He didn't want to have this discussion in front of Dave, but he was not going to drop the subject. He would get the answer from her later. Picking up the pen, he signed the rest of the paperwork.

"Here, look at this." Darcy turned the laptop so they could all see. A beautiful picture of the ranch filled the screen. A small paragraph describing the ranch and the beautiful scenery overlaid the picture. At the top, Tim had installed tabs to click on for information about the services offered, costs, and scheduling.

"Wow. Tim did a great job." Ben clicked on all the options, amazed at how easy Tim had made the process of booking. "And you did a great job working out the fees."

Her eyes danced with excitement. "We can probably be up and running by next week. All that's lacking is the inspection and the permits."

"Excuse me for butting in, Darcy," said Dave, "but how are you going to have the time to conduct trail rides and do your job?"

"For now, I'll just do trail rides two days a week. I may be able to do a few afternoons here or there, depending on my work schedule." Darcy started gathering the signed documents and placing them into the appropriate folders.

"I'm wondering how a business that is only open a couple days a week is going to stay in business."

Darcy's eyes darted to Ben, who glanced up from the computer. When he didn't say anything, she said, "Well, that's just a start. If we get busier, we can hire another guide."

Dave's doubt registered on his face. He seemed to be weighing his words carefully. "Don't get me wrong. I think you've done a good job so far, but I'm not sure you've completely thought this through."

Ben rushed to defend Darcy. "In what way? Darcy's worked hard to get everything we need."

"I'm not discounting that. All I'm saying is for a business to succeed, you need to give it your all, not a hit or miss to be worked in around other commitments. People need to know you'll be there when they want your services. Otherwise, they'll go somewhere else."

Ben picked at a hangnail on his thumb. "We can't afford to hire another guide until we see how things go."

Dave directed his comments to his brother. "Look, with Darcy only being available two days a week, I don't want the burden of this enterprise to fall on you. You simply can't take on more responsibilities."

Darcy's shoulders slumped. Without looking at either of them, she shut down the laptop and slid it into its case. "I've got to get back and deliver these documents before office hours this afternoon."

"I'll walk you out." Ben started to rise from his seat.

She held up a hand. "No, that's okay. I can see myself out." She grabbed everything from the table and hurried out the door before he could object.

He watched her retreating back. She had been so excited and bubbling over with enthusiasm when she'd arrived. Now her spark had completely gone out.

Dave sighed. "I'm sorry. I didn't mean to upset her."

Ben turned to him. "I thought you were on board with this. You didn't raise any objections yesterday."

"I know. I didn't want to say anything to put a damper on your idea. But the more I thought about it, the more concerned I became about how Darcy was going to manage two jobs. Her career as a vet obviously takes precedence." Dave tightened his jaw as if debating whether or not to continue. Then he looked away and said, "I don't mean to be a nay-sayer, but let's face it. This business is little more than a hobby for her. You're the one who stands to lose if this thing fails. You're the one with skin in the game."

Ben stood and paced the length of the kitchen, clenching and unclenching his fists. It wasn't as if he hadn't thought about the logistics of running a part-time side business. But Dave's words pushed those misgivings front and center where he'd been careful not to give them an audience.

"Forgive me if I'm out of line, little bro, but does this arrangement have anything to do with the fact the vet is an attractive young woman?"

Ben whirled around, anger rising in his gut. "No! Of course not! There's nothing between Darcy and me."

"Ben, come on, this is *me* you're talking to. I saw how you two looked at each other."

Ben held up his hands in frustration. "What? How did we look at each other?"

Dave let out a long breath. "The same way you used to look at Jolene."

Ben felt as though Dave had thrown a bucket of ice water in his face. "What? That's not true."

Dave rose and tried to put his arm around his brother's shoulder, but Ben shrugged him off. "You were infatuated with Jolene," he said, his voice soft. "I see the same thing happening with Darcy. And I'm wondering if you're just going along with this idea because it's what *she* wants, not what you want. Just like you used to do with Jolene. You gave her whatever she wanted."

Ben's nostrils flared and white-hot rage coursed through his veins. Stabbing his index finger at Dave's chest, he yelled, "You're *way* out of line, Dave!" He stomped to the kitchen door and continued outside. If he could have, he would have slammed the door behind him.

CHAPTER TWELVE

Ben needed to get away and clear his head. He walked briskly to the barn, where he saddled up Malachi, and headed out at a gallop. After several minutes of trying to outrun the conversation with his brother, he pulled up in front of a small brook that ran through the property. Dismounting, he let Malachi rest while he perched on a flat stone.

This place always soothed his troubled spirit. With the sound of the burbling water and the buzzing of nature all around him, Ben felt the presence of God more fully here than anywhere else. He wrapped his arms around his knees and rested his head against his arms, his eyes closed, just drinking in peace, and trying to let his anger diffuse.

He shouldn't have gotten so angry at Dave. After all, Ben was the one who asked Dave to stay because he wanted his brother's input. Dave had just been honest with him, and it wasn't that Ben hadn't had the same concern. *Had* he let Darcy's passion affect his judgment? He had to admit he was a little gun-shy after Jolene. But he had learned from that experience, hadn't he? Wasn't he stronger, smarter, and less gullible as far as letting his infatuation with a woman influence his good sense?

For that matter, how *did* he feel about Darcy? Was he infatuated with her? Reminding himself that Darcy was not Jolene, Ben took in a lungful of air and blew it out slowly, forcing himself to honestly evaluate where he stood with Darcy. Okay, he couldn't deny the attraction he felt to her. The racing of his pulse every time they were together certainly confirmed he had more on his mind than a mere business relationship. His brain might say one thing, but his heart disagreed. Still, infatuation didn't describe how he felt about Darcy. His feelings ran deeper than mere infatuation. Darcy was honest and good and reliable—the real deal. She was a giver, not a taker.

Ben raised his head and stared out at the water. He'd vowed never again to let a woman get close to him. So how had Darcy managed to get under his skin without even trying? And, more importantly, what, if anything, should he do about it? Did he dare take a risk at cracking open his heart again? Romantic relationships didn't mix well with business. Could he keep his feelings for her strictly platonic? That would be difficult if faced with seeing her several times a week. Still, he would have to figure out a way to keep his distance. At this point, they were in too far to scrap the whole venture, and the business had to come first. Besides, despite what Dave said, Darcy was the one who had done all the work and put up all the capital to get the business up and running. Ben had to admit he was almost as excited about the whole idea as she was.

He lowered his head once more and let his heart speak to God. "Please, Lord, show me the way." Although no audible words came from above, a supernatural peace flowed over and around him. Ben didn't know how everything would work out, but he had confidence it would.

Ben found Dave working on the porch when he rode back. Without saying a word, he picked up a hammer and began working alongside his brother. They labored side-by-side until Dave finally broke the silence.

"I'm sorry, Ben. This whole trail-riding enterprise is none of my business. I abandoned the ranch and my right to interfere with its operation a long time ago. You need to run it as you see fit."

Ben stopped hammering and locked eyes with his brother. "No, Dave. You didn't abandon the ranch. You just chose a different course, that's all. One that was right for you. But that doesn't mean you don't have a say in what happens to the ranch. Besides, I was the one who asked for your opinion, and I appreciate your honesty. It wasn't your fault I didn't like what you had to say."

A smile tugged at Dave's lips. "I guess I can't get past being the big brother no matter how old you are. I just want to look out for you. I sometimes forget you're perfectly capable of looking out for yourself."

Ben nodded. "I appreciate that, too." He breathed out a heavy sigh. "But you know what? I think this time I'll be okay."

"I think so, too."

"Darcy, could you come into my office for a minute?"

Dr. Tippins' summons stirred up jitters in Darcy's belly. He didn't sound pleased.

"Yes, sir." She clasped her suddenly sweaty hands together to keep them from shaking and stepped into his office, where her boss sat at his desk, rocking back and forth in his leather chair.

In his early sixties, Dr. Tippins still maintained a commanding presence. Tall and muscular, with a full head of silver hair and piercing blue eyes, his quiet strength generally instilled confidence in those around him. Except for when he was angry, as he appeared to be now. "Close the door."

Uh-oh. Darcy tried to pre-empt her boss' rebuke. "I apologize for being late, sir. I got hung up at the lawyer's office."

Dr. Tippins stared at her over the top of his bifocals while she squirmed inwardly. He didn't say anything for several agonizing seconds. Finally, he looked away from her and sighed. "Darcy, what you do on your own time is strictly your business. But when it starts affecting your job, then it becomes *my* business."

Darcy nodded and gulped. She had been late several times in the past few weeks while running around in circles taking care of all the necessary steps to make Whispering Winds Trail Rides a reality. Dave's words echoed in her ears. Had she bitten off more than she could chew? Would she be able to manage both her job as a veterinarian and her pipedream with Ben?

But with everything pretty much in place now, her schedule should be less erratic. She knew her boss, however, didn't want to hear about her outside interest. He just wanted a reliable veterinarian, and she had to admit she had been shirking her duty lately.

"Yes, sir." She raised her nervous eyes from the floor daring to meet his intense gaze for a fraction of a second before lowering them again.

"I hired you to practice veterinary medicine. Not to give trail rides."

"Yes, sir."

"If this outside work continues to affect your job here, I will have no alternative but to terminate your employment. I don't need to remind you that you are still in your six-month probation period."

A burning panic constricted Darcy's chest. She couldn't lose her job. Tears stung her eyes, and she willed herself not to cry. A woman who couldn't maintain control of her emotions was the last thing Dr. Tippins needed. Blinking rapidly to clear away the tears, she said, "I understand, sir, and I promise I will do better."

His eyes softened slightly. "I hope so, Darcy. You're a good veterinarian and I would hate to lose you." He rose and grabbed his hat from his desk. "I've got calls to make and you have a waiting room full of appointments to see. I suggest you get busy."

CHAPTER THIRTEEN

"Ben! We've got bookings!" Darcy's excited voice carried through the phone.

"Already? That's amazing. The website's only been live for a day."

Darcy laughed. "Well, look at our client list."

She waited while he brought up the website, then heard him chuckling. "Our Sunday school class?"

"Yes. I wonder who put them up to it. Tim? Molly?"

"Doesn't matter. We have clients. Pre-paid clients, no less."

"Maybe we should schedule the ride for a Sunday afternoon and have a potluck picnic at the ranch."

"That's a great idea. And you know what? This calls for a celebration. How about I take you out for a congratulatory pizza tonight?"

Darcy's heart skipped a beat. "I'd like that."

"Great. Is seven o'clock okay? I'll pick you up."

"Perfect. See you then." Darcy swiped the end call button and sat for a long moment cocooned in warm fuzzies. *Don't go there, Darcy*, a little voice in her head warned. *Keep your relationship strictly professional.* The warning threatened to put a damper on her exuberant mood. "Nope, negative thoughts, you're not going to ruin this day," she said aloud.

With her body already tingling with the thrill of the business becoming a reality, she permitted herself to explore the forbidden feelings she had developed for Ben. But when she lifted the lid to that Pandora's box, she found she'd unleashed a myriad of emotions she had tried hard to tamp down, and there was no way to shove them back into the box.

Would a personal relationship with him be completely out of the question? The thought filled her with a sense of giddiness she hadn't experienced in a long time. Ben was a wonderful man—honest, kind, and considerate, not to mention incredibly good-looking. Although she knew looks only ran so deep, Ben's striking blue eyes and unruly dark hair only enhanced his inner qualities. But could a professional and personal relationship coexist? Darcy had to admit she might be ready to take the risk and explore the possibility. Josh had hurt her deeply, but she couldn't allow her pain to define the rest of her life. She didn't want to go through life wounded and bitter, afraid to love again.

But one roadblock lay ahead—Ben. At times, she sensed he had feelings for her too, and perhaps wanted more from her. But he might be just as scared as she was. After what Molly told her about Jolene, Darcy could understand his reluctance to trust someone else and risk getting burned again. Plus, he had never talked about Jolene with her. Tonight. She would test the waters with him tonight and see where they led.

"You look nice," said Ben, when Darcy answered his knock on her door. His approval shone in his eyes.

"It's just a pair of jeans and a sweater," she replied, secretly pleased by his compliment. She would never tell him how she had agonized over her choice of clothing for tonight. Wanting to appear casual, yet classy, she had considered and discarded several outfits before deciding on the white jeans and red sweater. He had seen her several times at her most unattractive, in her baggy brown coveralls and steel-toed boots, but tonight, Darcy wanted him to see her as a feminine woman, not as a horse wrangler.

"You look good, yourself," she said, taking in his khakis and button-down blue shirt. Outside of church, she had only ever seen him in worn blue jeans.

He leaned in for a side hug, and she caught a whiff of musky cologne. Hmm. Hadn't noticed *that* before, either. Even at church. "Are you ready to go?" he asked.

"Yes, I'm starving." Darcy locked her door and dropped the key into her purse. She preceded him down the narrow walkway, but as they neared the parking lot, she felt his hand on the small of her back leading her to his truck. His touch sent a shiver down her spine.

Okay, enough pretending. You're falling for him. Maybe more than falling. Darcy willed her pattering heart to slow down, but it refused to obey. If she put herself out there and her feelings weren't reciprocated, the comfortable relationship they now shared would be strained. Was it worth taking that chance?

Sitting next to him in his truck, she became more aware of his masculine presence than ever before. His arms, tanned and muscular, gripped the steering wheel with relaxed composure. He glanced her way and smiled, and Darcy felt her knees go weak.

Stop it! It wasn't as if she hadn't been in close proximity to him for several weeks now. But since she'd allowed herself to consider opening the door beyond friendship, her body was reacting in embarrassing and unpredictable ways. *Darcy, get hold of yourself! You're not a character in a romance novel, for heaven's sake.* She tried to concentrate on what he was saying but found herself noticing for perhaps the first time how broad his shoulders were and how soft, yet strong his lips appeared.

As they pulled up to the pizza joint and he assisted her from the truck, Darcy acknowledged she was seeing him through a whole new set of eyes, and it was making her more and more uneasy. With every fiber of willpower she possessed, she tried to compose herself. She didn't want to fall apart now and make a complete fool of herself, like some teenager with a crush.

Forcing herself to appear normal, she made it through the dinner, although her stomach rebelled at the few bites she managed to choke down. Finally, she pushed her plate away and sighed.

"Are you okay?" Ben asked. "You said you were starving, but you've hardly eaten a thing, and you've seemed preoccupied all evening."

Darcy tried to brush his question aside. "Just nerves, I guess." She quickly added, "I mean, I'm excited about our business being operational."

He narrowed his eyes and studied her. She looked away, unable to hold his gaze.

"Is something else bothering you, Darcy?" His tone was gentle.

She compressed her lips and took in a breath. "Ben, can I ask you something?" She brought her eyes back to his and saw concern in them. The last thing she wanted to do at this point was make him think she had second thoughts about the partnership they'd just formed.

"I guess so." He placed an elbow on the table and rested his cheek against his palm, a gesture he had done so often in the past. She found it endearing, as it meant she had his undivided attention.

It was now or never. With her heart hammering against her ribs, she said, "Would you tell me about Jolene?"

He sat up straight, his eyes widening in surprise. Then he closed them and shook his head before returning his eyes to hers. "Okay, I did not see that coming."

A thread of remorse tugged at Darcy's conscience for asking him to share a painful episode in his life. "I'm sorry. You don't have to tell me anything if you don't want to. It's none of my business. It's just–"

"I know. It's a small town. People talk."

She nodded.

He blew out a humorless laugh. "You've probably heard most of the story anyway."

"Some," she admitted.

"Why do you want to know about her?"

Darcy bit her lip. How honest should she be? *Because I want to know everything about you. Because I want for us to take our relationship deeper, but I have to know where you've been to do so. Because I can't be part of your future if you're still stuck in the past.*

Reaching across the table, she laid her hand over his. "I care about you, Ben. I want to know more about you." A safe and, hopefully, vague enough answer to put her toes in the water, yet not jump in over her head.

He fixed his eyes on her but seemed to see beyond her, focused somewhere far away. Taking a long breath through his nose, he forced the air out slowly over his flattened lips. "Jolene. Okay. Where do I start?"

She remained quiet, allowing him to collect his thoughts.

"Let me skip to the punch line and say I made a huge mistake right from the beginning." Now his gaze locked on something over her shoulder. "I met Jolene when I went out to help an older lady, Miss Maudie, fix her roof after a storm. Some shingles had come loose, and she knows she can always call on me for minor repairs. Miss Maudie is the salt of the earth. There's nothing I wouldn't do for that sweet lady."

Touched by his unselfishness and willingness to help an old woman in need, Darcy smiled but doubted Ben noticed.

"Anyway, I was up on the roof hammering away when this woman came out onto the front porch looking like she was about to rip me a new one for making so much noise. She looked up, and my heart just froze. She was the most beautiful woman I had ever seen."

His words caused an unexpected blow to her female ego. Even though Molly had told her Jolene was fashion-model gorgeous, hearing Ben confirm it only rubbed salt into a new wound she didn't even realize she had until she felt the sting. Darcy thought about the first time Ben had seen *her*. What a contrast.

"Suddenly, the anger on her face just melted away and she said, 'Hi, I'm Jolene, Miss Maudie's great-niece.' I was so tongue-tied that I couldn't say anything. She was wearing short cut-offs and a cropped top, and boy, did she have a great figure." He paused, a sheepish grin on his face. "Well, let's just say I'm a guy. I took notice."

Darcy's self-esteem plummeted even lower. She suddenly wondered if she really wanted him to continue.

"I don't even know what else she said. All I knew was my brain had turned to mush and I couldn't think straight. I'm not sure how I finished up the roof, but somehow my body knew the drill since my brain had shut down. All the time I worked, she kept glancing up at me with this flirty look.

"When I got done, Miss Maudie came out on the porch and invited me in for a cold drink. While we were sitting around the table, she mentioned that my family owned Whispering Winds Ranch. Jolene jumped all over that. She asked all kinds of questions about the ranch—what it looked like, what we did, what kind of animals we had—and the next thing I knew, I had invited her out to see it." He shook his head. "I asked her to go riding with me the first time she visited the ranch."

"Kind of like me?" Darcy asked, a thread of jealousy in her tone.

Ben snorted. "Not hardly. Jolene didn't know the first thing about horses. And me . . . well, I just wanted to impress her with all my expertise, and I wanted to take care of her, you know? Jolene was tiny and fragile, the epitome of the helpless little woman." He rolled his eyes. "Boy, she could play that part to perfection. Stupid me, I loved playing the part of her hero. I was so infatuated with her that I didn't pay any attention to all the red flags."

Darcy perked up a little. Did *she* have red flags she was waving under Ben's nose? "Like what?"

Ben sighed. "Like the fact she really didn't like the horses or the cows. Or even Mack, for that matter."

"Mack? How could anybody not like Mack?"

His mouth turned up at the corners, but the smile didn't quite reach his eyes. "Let's just say she was a delicate little flower who didn't like getting her hands dirty."

Darcy nodded and fiddled with her silverware. Not getting her hands dirty certainly didn't apply to *her*. Not with what she did every day. How did Ben feel about *that*? Did it make her less feminine in his eyes?

"Then there were her expensive tastes. Jolene could be quite the aristocrat. She had this way of cajoling me into buying the things she coveted. And nothing but the best restaurants. At the time, I didn't realize the ranch was not doing well financially. I thought we had plenty of money, so I didn't mind spoiling Jolene if it made her happy. She had me hooked so fast I had a hard time keeping up."

He took a long sip of his water and let his gaze wander around the noisy pizza parlor. "The next thing I knew we were engaged." He shook his head. "I'm still not quite sure how that happened. Everything moved so quickly. I honestly don't remember proposing, but suddenly, there we were, picking out an engagement ring."

Darcy listened, feeling more unsettled by the moment, almost sorry she had started down this painful road.

"After we got engaged, her church attendance

became more erratic. She had started going with me at first, but then she seemed to lose interest. Then, when my dad died unexpectedly . . ." His voice became thick, and his eyes misted.

She squeezed his hand. "I'm sorry. That must have been devastating for you."

He swallowed hard and rubbed a hand across his eyes. "The worst. But it was almost as if . . . I hate to voice this thought aloud. I've never shared this thought with anyone."

Darcy waited. When he didn't say anything, she said, "That's okay, you don't have to."

Without acknowledging that she had spoken, he went on. "It was almost as if Jolene was glad. Now I owned everything, and she would be the mistress of the ranch."

Darcy gasped and clasped her hand over her mouth.

Ben huffed out a mirthless laugh. "Well, that dream didn't last long. After suffering huge losses in two freak storms and discovering the ranch bled red ink, she decided that 'for richer or poorer' didn't really work for her unless it was for richer. She broke the engagement and left before Dad was cold in his grave."

"Wow." The impact of Jolene's greed and heartlessness touched a nerve deep in Darcy's core. "Where is she now?"

He shrugged. "I have no idea. I guess she went back to wherever she came from. She never talked much about her past and, fool that I was, I never pushed her about it."

"I'm so sorry, Ben." Her eyes sought his, but his eyes still looked into another dimension, far away from the boisterous crowd surrounding them.

"The thing is, I failed to see anything below Jolene's surface. People tried to warn me, but I was too blinded by her beauty and her beguiling ways. When I finally opened my eyes, I couldn't believe what a complete chump I had been."

"At least you found out before you married her."

He nodded slowly. "Yes, I praise God for that. I think He protected me."

"Thank you for telling me, Ben. I'm sorry for bringing up a painful subject."

He turned his attention back to her. "It's okay. So now you know the whole, sordid story. If that wasn't a downer to what was supposed to be a celebration, I don't know what is."

His story had failed to bring her the reassurance she had hoped for to move the relationship forward. For some unexplainable reason, Darcy found herself envying the other woman who had managed to capture Ben's heart so completely. Despite their relationship not working out, Darcy knew Ben would never view *her* as the helpless little woman he wanted to take care of. Not that she wanted or needed a man to take care of her. But if that was the type of woman he was attracted to, Darcy could never fit into that stereotype.

She knew Ben admired her strength and self-sufficiency, but sometimes those traits seemed threatening to a man who was looking for a needier, more dependent woman. As a business partner, strong traits were important. As a romantic partner . . . Well, some men just needed to be, as Ben said, the hero. It was hard to flex your muscles and impress a woman who matched your own strength. Independent women might be a turn-off for him. She found his revelation disappointing. It meant she was not the type of woman who attracted him, and he could never have more interest in her than as a friend and business partner.

She couldn't declare her feelings for him now, knowing they wouldn't be returned. It would ruin everything, and she would be humiliated. No mutual attraction existed between them. He was simply a nice man whom she had misread. Her heart squeezed with this knowledge. She would just have to put her personal feelings aside and concentrate on her work.

"It was my fault for asking." Forcing a smile, she said, "Let's talk about more pleasant topics. Like the picnic and trail ride Sunday."

CHAPTER FOURTEEN

Sunday dawned bright and clear, with wispy white clouds in a brilliant blue sky. A gentle breeze carried the clean scent of freshly mown grass, a chore Ben had performed yesterday in preparation for the picnic. He had scrubbed the two wooden picnic tables and moved them closer to the house, where food could be carried back and forth from the kitchen.

It would be nice to have a group of people at the ranch again. They hadn't entertained much since before Mom died. But he remembered the large gatherings of friends who frequented the many social events they used to hold. Those had been some of the best times in his life. All the good times seemed to have slipped away in the grief following his mother's death, and later the busyness of trying to run the ranch on his own.

Ben ducked out quickly after church to finish setting up before everyone arrived. He had to admit he was looking forward to the inauguration of Whispering Winds Trail Rides, even if it was just his Sunday school class. It had been way too long since he'd spent a relaxing day just enjoying the company of good friends.

He whistled as he removed the hamburgers and hotdogs from the freezer and set them on the kitchen counter to thaw. Then he pulled two large pitchers from the cabinet and mixed up pitchers of lemonade and iced tea. After setting the pitchers in the refrigerator to chill, he stepped outside to make sure he had everything ready for the grill. Not seeing his favorite spatula, he walked back into the kitchen and searched through his utensil drawer. He had hoped Darcy would be here to help him set up, but she'd said she needed to go home and change clothes first.

Mack's barking alerted him to the first arriving guests. Ben recognized Tim's black Explorer bouncing over the gravel, with Molly and Kendra in the cab next to him. Mack greeted the group as the truck stopped near the house. Molly and Kendra climbed out of the passenger door, each bearing a covered bowl.

"Here, Ben." Molly thrust a blue bowl into his hands. "This needs to go in the refrigerator until time to eat. It's potato salad."

"Mine, too," said Kendra, handing him a clear bowl with what looked like fresh fruit.

Ben balanced the bowls in one arm while struggling to open the screen door. Mack continued to bark. "Mack, knock it off," Ben called out through the partially open door.

Tim followed Ben into the kitchen, bearing a brown grocery bag. "Where do you want the buns?"

"Just set them anywhere. Where are the ladies?"

"Checking out the stable. They're really excited about the trail ride. That's all they talked about on the way over." Tim set the bag on the table and removed several packs of buns. "This is a nice place."

With a pang of guilt, it dawned on Ben that he had never invited any of his church friends to his home.

"Thanks. We need to do this more often." He glanced at the packages of bread Tim had bought. "Whoa, how many people were you expecting?"

Tim shrugged. "I never know how much stuff to buy."

"By the way, the website turned out great. I can't tell you how much we appreciate it."

"It was fairly straightforward. I was glad to help."

Ben wanted to ask how much the website cost, knowing that Darcy had already paid Tim. He had never been able to get her to tell him the price, and he wanted to reimburse her. But there was no subtle way to bring the subject up with Tim, and Ben knew it would only irritate her if he did.

Besides, Darcy had been acting strange the past few days, ever since their pizza night. He didn't know what had changed between them, but he felt a distinct distancing on her part. Was it something he had said about Jolene? That didn't make sense, as Darcy was the one who had asked about her. He dismissed the idea. She was probably just busy with everything she had to do.

He had to hand it to her. She had been out to the ranch multiple times, riding and evaluating each horse's personality and temperament to better match them to the riders for which they would be most suitable. Although he hadn't been able to accompany her, he enjoyed seeing her here and had gotten used to her presence. It seemed as if she belonged here.

Mack barked again, as the sound of another vehicle coming up the drive grabbed Ben's attention. Tim poked his head out the door and announced, "There's Bill and Audrey."

A prick of disappointment that it wasn't Darcy tugged at Ben's awareness. Where was she, anyway?

"Uh, Ben, you do know I've never ridden a horse before, right?" Tim's hesitant voice forced Ben back into the moment.

"No kidding? And you've lived in Wyoming how long?" Ben teased.

Uneasiness spread over Tim's face. "All my life. But I'm a city boy and a tech nerd."

"Well, I promise not to laugh at your horsemanship if you promise not to laugh at my computer skills. Or perhaps I should say my lack of computer skills."

"Not quite the same. Nobody ever got killed using a computer."

Ben chuckled. "Maybe not. Unless you count the number of people who commit suicide over their frustration with technology."

Tim pushed his glasses up on the bridge of his nose. "Yeah, well, tell Darcy to take it easy on me, okay? No galloping and jumping over fences."

Ben slung his arm over Tim's shoulder. "Don't worry. She's an expert. She'll have you on the slowest, most gentle horse in the stable, and she'll walk with you."

Tim still didn't look so sure, but Bill and Audrey interrupted the conversation by bursting into the kitchen, their arms loaded.

"Here's the baked beans. Do you want them in here or on the table outside?" Still holding a blue-and-white casserole dish, Audrey reached up to swipe an errant strand of black hair out of her face with her elbow.

"You can set them here. I figured we could dish up in the kitchen and then take our plates outside to eat."

"Speaking of dishes, I've got the paper plates and utensils," said Bill, setting two plastic bags on the table.

"Yeah, Mr. 'I Don't Cook.' Let the women do all the work while all you do is buy paper plates," Audrey teased.

Bill grinned. "Trust me, you don't want me to cook. Anyway, *somebody* had to bring plates. It's hard to eat baked beans out of your hands."

Audrey rolled her eyes. "Where's Darcy?"

"Not here yet," said Ben.

Audrey frowned. "She'd better get here soon. There's no way I'm riding a horse until the expert shows up to teach me how."

"And there's no way I'm riding a horse until I eat," said Tim. "It could be my last meal."

They all laughed. "I didn't realize what a bunch of city slickers you all were," said Ben.

"Who's a city slicker?" said Molly, as she and Kendra joined the group. "I'll have you know I took first place in barrel racing when I was sixteen."

"Good, that's one of you I won't have to worry about." Ben grabbed the platter of hot dogs and hamburgers. "I'm going to start the grill."

They all gravitated outside and chatted while Ben cooked. But Darcy still hadn't appeared by the time he pulled everything off the grill.

"Should we wait for Darcy?" asked Kendra.

"Maybe we should try to call her," said Molly. She pulled her phone out of her pocket, scrolled through her contact list, and held the phone to her ear. "Hmm. Goes straight to voice mail. She must not have turned her phone back on after church."

A small twinge of worry lodged in Ben's gut, but

then, to his relief, he saw Darcy's truck pulling in.

"It's about time," chided Molly, when Darcy emerged from her truck.

"Sorry, I got hung up at the clinic."

"I thought you weren't on call today," said Ben.

"I'm not, but I had a patient to check on. It took longer than I anticipated." She didn't meet his eyes.

Ben scrutinized her for a long moment. Dressed in form-fitting jeans, a loose T-shirt that read "Fuller Farms Riding Academy," and riding boots, with her hair pulled back in its ubiquitous ponytail, she appeared capable, as well as adorable. But something seemed off about her. The bubbly spark that defined her had been absent for a few days.

He wondered if something had happened. This should be a joyful day for all of them. Maybe the animal she'd had to check on had more problems than she'd expected, but the change in her had occurred before today. Maybe he could get her alone and talk later. If something was wrong, he wanted to know.

Ben found his heart aching for whatever it was that had doused her enthusiasm. Part of his attraction to her was her infectious passion for everything around her, and it pained him to think she was hurting in some way and didn't feel comfortable sharing with him—particularly after he bared his soul to her the other night. The same sensation of protectiveness he'd felt for Jolene washed over him, and he cautioned himself to squelch it.

Despite his ever-increasing feelings for Darcy—and he had to admit those feelings were taking on a life of their own—he couldn't fix everything for her. Wanting to play the hero came naturally to him, but he had to remind himself that he couldn't be the hero all the time. Besides, Darcy was not the kind of woman who would welcome a knight in shining armor rushing in to save the day. If anything, that kind of response would push her further away.

Ben didn't understand what had gone wrong between them. He'd allowed himself a sliver of hope for something more to develop in their relationship, and he'd thought he'd sensed the same reaction from her. They both seemed to be cautiously feeling their way with each other. But maybe he'd been mistaken. Maybe he'd misinterpreted her openness and friendliness as attraction for him. If she realized his growing attraction for her and didn't feel the same for him, she might be uncomfortable around him, especially considering how closely they would be working together. Then again, whatever was bothering her might have nothing to do with him at all.

Ben tried to shake off his apprehension so he could enjoy the day. "Who's hungry?" he asked, forcing cheerfulness into his voice.

His question was met with hearty enthusiasm and a bustling of activity as everyone headed for the kitchen, leaving him holding a platter of burgers and hot dogs. Darcy remained planted in the same spot.

"Oh, I forgot," she said, turning back to the truck. "I brought brownies."

"Sounds good." He waited while she retrieved the dessert from the front seat.

She smiled. "Don't say that until you taste them. I'm not the best cook. But you can hardly go wrong with packaged brownie mix."

Ah, her smile was back. He allowed himself to relax

a little and stop speculating on whatever he imagined to be a problem.

The afternoon couldn't have turned out better. After lunch, everyone headed to the stable where Ben, Darcy, and Molly had the horses saddled and ready to go in no time. Darcy assigned the horses she thought would best fit the needs of the rider. Then, with her leading and Ben bringing up the rear, the group set off for a leisurely ride. Even Tim seemed to have a good time once he learned how to stop his horse from veering off to eat grass.

"Jasper knows an amateur when he sees one." Ben chuckled. "Pull on one rein and give him a little kick."

"Yeah, Tim, you have to be smarter than the horse," said Molly.

Darcy turned around in her saddle. "You all stop picking on Tim. He's doing great for his first time on a horse."

"And last," muttered Tim.

"No way," said Ben. "I'm thinking about making a trail ride a regular outing for our group."

"Maybe we could just stick to bowling," said Tim.

Bill piped up. "You're not any better at bowling."

"Yeah, but at least I stand less chance of being injured unless I drop the ball on my foot. Besides, after today, I'm not sure I'll ever be able to walk again."

They continued along at an unhurried pace, with Ben pointing out different areas of the ranch. The group enjoyed seeing the grazing cattle, especially the cows with their calves, but they stayed well away from the animals. At Ben's favorite spot by the brook, they stopped for a break.

Tim dismounted, walked a few bow-legged steps, and said, "Do I really have to get back on that beast? Couldn't I just walk from here?"

"You could, but it's a long walk." Ben undid his backpack and passed around water bottles.

"I want to get my feet wet," said Molly. "Who's with me?"

Whoops of laughter erupted from the gang, and in no time, they were playing and splashing in the water like a bunch of children. Darcy stood by the bank.

"Don't you want to come in?" Ben called to her.

She shook her head. "I'll just stay here with the horses."

"They'll be fine. They're not going anywhere. Come on in."

Soon everyone was urging her to join them, so she finally sat on the grass and tugged off her boots and socks. Rolling up her jeans to below her knees, she stepped gingerly into the cold stream.

"The water's freezing!" she cried, as she raised one foot, then alternated with the other.

"Oh, come on, Darcy, even Tim isn't complaining," said Kendra.

"What is this, 'pick on Tim day'?" Tim retorted. "As a matter of fact, I'm a very good swimmer. I'm not a complete nerd, you know."

"Too bad the water isn't deep enough to make you prove it," said Molly.

"Well, be that as it may, I'm not stupid enough to swim in ice water."

Darcy picked her way over slippery rocks to where

the rest of the group stood in the middle of the stream, the frigid water swirling around their legs. Just as she reached the others, her foot slipped on a moss-covered rock and she went over backwards. Strong arms grabbed her before she hit the water.

"Careful, we don't want to lose our leader. We might never make it back to civilization."

Darcy looked up into Ben's grinning face and felt heat rising in her body, despite the chilly water. He held her for way longer than necessary and she let him, her eyes mesmerized by his intense blue gaze. It wasn't until the amused rumblings of the rest of the gang reached her ears that she released the stranglehold she hadn't even realized she had on Ben.

Clearing her throat, she said, "I'm okay now. I'm just a little klutzy."

He continued to hold her. "Come on. I'll help you back to the shore."

She opened her mouth to say she could make it, but he had his arm around her waist and she decided not to protest. Leaning against his strong chest felt too good.

Once back on dry ground, he hovered over her. "Are you sure you're all right? You didn't sprain your ankle or anything, did you?"

Darcy laughed. "Ben, I'm fine. I just slipped. Nothing is hurt but my pride. And fortunately, you spared me the embarrassment of going through the rest of the day with soaked pants." She barely noticed the rest of the gang making their way back.

Everyone dried off and remounted their horses for the rest of the ride. Back at the house, they ate a cold supper of leftovers, then Ben started a fire in the fire pit behind the house. Molly grabbed some blankets from the truck, while Bill brought out his guitar.

"Shoot, we should have brought marshmallows," said Audrey.

"I'm too full to eat another thing," said Kendra.

Ben poked at the fire, then plopped down on the blanket next to Darcy.

So much for keeping my distance. She had tried maintaining her distance for the last several days, but she'd been miserable, and she knew Ben was wondering why she was acting so strangely. She'd had every intention of keeping her barriers in place today, knowing they would be interacting closely. She had purposefully come late to the picnic, not wanting to be alone with Ben. But when she slipped and he caught her in the stream, all her defenses came crashing down.

It was no use. She was hopelessly smitten. Staying away from him had not helped. Her heart had a mind of its own and she couldn't rein it in from wandering where it wanted to go. How she could continue working so intimately with Ben while living with the gnawing ache in her gut of knowing he would never see her as anyone other than a friend, she didn't know. But for now, she would pretend he returned her feelings. The fantasy brought joy to her spirit.

The clear, dusky sky came alive with shimmering stars and a half-moon. Bill strummed his guitar and they sang sweet praise songs while the dancing fire created fanciful shadows all around them. Even Mack lay contentedly on the edge of the blanket enjoying the evening. Darcy leaned back on her elbows and simply relished the moment. If only . . . She shivered.

"You're cold," Ben said, removing his jacket and placing it around her shoulders.

She sat up and pulled his jacket around herself, breathing in the scent of horse mixed with Ben's musky cologne. How she longed to lean against his shoulder like she had earlier in the creek. Then, suddenly, he scooted closer to her, placing his arm around her and pulling her against him. Her heart did flip-flops, and she feared he would hear it thumping around in her chest. *Stop reading so much into his gesture. He's just being a gentleman because you're cold.*

As complete darkness settled around them, the fire slowly began to die down. Finally, Bill put his guitar aside and stood. "Well, I'm afraid that's it for me. I've got to be up early in the morning."

"Me, too," chorused several of the others. In no time, the blankets were folded, dishes were gathered, and people were saying good night to each other. Darcy turned to leave as well.

"Darcy, wait," said Ben, laying a hand on her arm as the others piled into their vehicles and headed out.

She paused, looking up into his face. The magic night had come to an end. Time to get back to reality. "I really should be going, too."

He searched her eyes for a long time. "Are you sure everything's okay? You've not been yourself these last few days."

Darcy forced a smile. "Yes, of course. I'm fine. Just a little tired, that's all."

"Today was wonderful. Everybody had a great time. You really did it, Darcy. Whispering Winds Trail Rides is officially open."

"*We* did it. Not just me."

"Well, I do know none of this would have happened without you. Which is why" . . . He paused.

"Yes?" Her eyes sought his with expectation. Could she dare to hope that perhaps she was wrong about him?

He shook his head. "Nothing." He bent down and placed a chaste kiss on her cheek. "Good night."

Although her cheek burned where he had planted his kiss against it, her spirits sank. "Good night."

CHAPTER FIFTEEN

Darcy stepped out of the shower after washing away the smell of wood smoke and horse, the scent of Ben's musky cologne from his jacket still in her nose. Although exhausted, her body was wound up with the emotions she'd been struggling with all day. How long could she keep riding this roller coaster of ups and downs?

For a little while tonight, she had thought Ben might be having feelings for her, too. He had obviously wanted to say something to her but then changed his mind at the last minute. As she wrapped a towel around her wet hair, she heard the chirping of her cell phone in the bedroom. Ben! Maybe he'd gotten up the courage to say whatever had been on his mind earlier.

She grabbed the phone and said, "Ben?"

A short pause ensued. "Uh, no, Darcy, it's Josh. Who's Ben?"

Her heart sputtered. She hadn't checked the caller ID. Why hadn't she blocked Josh's number? Ignoring his question, she said, "What do you want, Josh?" Glancing at the clock, she realized it was two hours later in Pennsylvania. Why was he calling so late? Couldn't sleep? Guilty conscience?

"I want to talk to you, Dar. You've not returned any of my calls."

And I wouldn't have answered this one if I'd known it was you. "We don't have anything to talk about, Josh." She sank onto the bed.

"Dar, please." His tone held carefully controlled desperation. "I miss you. I love you."

She snorted. "What happened to Zoe?" She hated the bitterness creeping into her voice, but she couldn't help herself.

Josh released a long sigh that carried through the phone. "That's over. It should never have begun in the first place, and I can't tell you how sorry I am."

Darcy pinched her lips. "You're right, it shouldn't have."

"You have every right to be angry with me. I messed up big time. But the minute I lost you, I knew you were the only one I ever loved. I knew what a horrible mistake I'd made."

"Kind of figured that out a little too late, didn't you?"

"Dar, please. I understand. It's just that . . . well, I guess I got a little nervous about the whole wedding thing and I went a little crazy."

"Is that your excuse? Temporary insanity?" She yanked the towel from her hair and threw it into the bathroom.

"It's not an excuse. I'm just trying to explain what happened."

"I *know* what happened, Josh, I was there. Remember?"

Another sigh sounded in her ear. "Look Dar—"

She gritted her teeth. "Don't call me Dar." She

couldn't stand to hear his pet nickname for her that had once been endearing but now sounded trite and meaningless.

"Sorry. Darcy. I'm asking you to forgive me."

Darcy tamped down her anger and tried to invoke a gentler frame of mind. Taking a calming breath and softening her tone, she replied, "I have forgiven you, Josh."

"Thanks, Darcy, I know I don't deserve your forgiveness, but I do appreciate it." Relief colored his voice.

No, you don't deserve it, but Jesus said we have to forgive. So, I did. There! That square's filled. The resentment still lodged in her chest belied her thoughts and words.

"So," he said in a tentative voice, "does this mean you would consider giving me another chance?"

She huffed. "No, Josh, that ship has sailed. Forgiveness is one thing. Opening myself up to have my heart trampled on again is another."

"Dar . . . Darcy, I would never do that again. I've learned my lesson."

"Good, then maybe you won't repeat the same mistake with another woman." She walked into the bathroom, retrieved the wet towel she'd hurled, and hung it over the towel rack.

"Please, Darcy, you're the only woman I want. The only woman I've ever wanted."

She didn't reply. He had a funny way of showing she was the only woman he'd ever wanted when he'd dumped her for Zoe. But she wasn't going to keep rubbing his nose in that fact.

"Darcy, I swear if you'll give me another chance,

I'll spend the rest of my life making it up to you for what I did. Please, Darcy. Come home and let's work things out between us."

Come home! "Josh, I *am* home. I live in Wyoming now."

"No, Darcy, Caryville is your home. You grew up here. Your family and friends are here. Your parents' work is here. You know how much you love Fuller Farms. How you always said you would take over the family business one day."

He had her there. She missed all the familiarity of home. She missed her parents and their business. But she had just started *her* new business. Her heart felt tugged in two directions. Still, even if she were to go home, she didn't want to start up anything with Josh. Though tempted, she could not go home where Josh would constantly be in her face, trying to wear her down—and where she would never see Ben again. She knew Ben could have her heart for the taking.

She ran a weary hand over her face. "Josh, I can't talk about this anymore right now. It's been a long day, and I'm tired."

"Okay," he said. "Just think about what I said. Please?"

"Yeah, whatever. I need to go." She pushed the end call button before he could say anything else. She sat on the edge of her bed, staring at the phone in her hand for a long time. How she wished she'd never talked to Josh. He'd managed to slip a toe in the door that she had tried so hard to firmly close.

CHAPTER SIXTEEN

"I'll be gone for the next few days," Ben said, as Darcy finished up a trail ride. "I've got to take some cattle to auction."

"Oh." A fleeting expression of disappointment crossed her face before she quickly replaced it with a smile. "That's a good thing."

"Yes, it is. It means I'll finally have some money coming in." He laughed. "Other than the gold mine of our trail riding business."

Her eyes shone. "I still can't believe how it's taken off. We're booked out for the next three weeks." She lugged a saddle to the barn.

He followed with an armload of tack. "I never would have thought we would do so well. I hope you're not overdoing it."

She carefully wiped down the saddle before placing it on the rack. "I'm loving every minute, but I do wish we could offer more bookings. I can only do so many."

Just then a voice came from the open door. "Excuse me?"

They turned to see a young woman with a honey-blonde bun on the top of her head, frizzy tendrils escaping and flowing freely around her flushed face.

"Yes?" said Ben.

The woman ventured into the area where Ben and Darcy worked.

"It's Olivia, isn't it?" said Darcy. "You were in the last group."

The woman offered a shy smile. "That's right. Olivia Anderson."

"What can we do for you?" asked Darcy.

Olivia shifted from one foot to the other. "Well, um, I was wondering if you might need help."

Ben and Darcy exchanged glances. "What kind of help?" Ben asked.

The young woman looked around as if to be sure she wasn't being overheard. "I work for Sumlin Stables in Jackson Hole. I've been there for two years. But the stable is under new management and, well . . ." She lowered her eyes, leaving the sentence unfinished.

"I take it you're not happy with the new management," said Ben.

"No. The manager keeps hitting on me."

"What?" cried Darcy. "That's sexual harassment. You should report his behavior."

Olivia shook her head and tears sprung to her eyes. "No, I . . . I really don't want to go through all that. It would be his word against mine. I just want to get out of there."

A slow burn rose in Ben's chest. Olivia should not have to quit her job because of the boorish behavior of the manager. The owner should be told. But it wasn't his decision. He understood how making serious accusations such as these against her boss could end up causing the poor girl more distress and humiliation.

"Besides, this place is much closer to my home."

"Where's your home?" asked Darcy.

"Just over in Colburn. A few miles."

"What kind of work do you do for Sumlin Stables?" said Ben.

"Trail rides. Riding lessons. But this place is much nicer. I, um, signed up today to check you out." She raised her eyes, and two spots of color rose in her pale cheeks.

Darcy smiled. "I'm glad we passed your scrutiny."

Olivia went on. "It took me a week to get scheduled. With all the tourists in Jackson Hole, you could do a lot better if you had more openings."

Ben looked at Darcy, then said to Olivia, "Could you give us a minute to talk privately?"

"Certainly." She hustled back outside as if afraid to overhear their conversation.

"What do you think?" Ben asked. "We were just talking about how busy we are. Do you think we should consider bringing someone else in?"

Darcy finished hanging up a bridle, taking her time before answering. "We could give it a try. Maybe on a probationary basis. She would obviously have to spend several days with me first."

He grinned. "Of course. You're the boss."

"I'll go tell her."

"That was one happy girl," Darcy told Ben after Olivia had gone. "Even when I explained her pay would be strictly on commission. She said that suited her fine."

"I just hope she can do the job." He washed his

hands in the outdoor sink and dried them on a dingy towel hanging on a hook over the sink.

"I'll watch her closely. I trained a lot of people at my parents' stable."

"I'll leave her in your capable hands. Anyway, as I was saying earlier, I'm going to be gone for a few days. Will you be able to handle the riding business by yourself?"

She smiled. "I pretty much do now, don't I?"

"Point taken. But if you need anything while I'm gone, Ricky will be here. I'm taking Cam with me."

"When do you leave?"

The odd look was back on her face, and he wondered if she would miss him. But that was silly. After all, with her work schedule, there were many days in which they didn't see each other. However, this trip seemed different. He didn't know why. A dull ache seized his belly, and he realized how much he was going to miss her. He wished he could have taken her with him, but she couldn't leave her job. Besides, it would be inappropriate for them to travel out of town together.

He thought about how he had become used to seeing her at the ranch, and how much he liked it. When he got back from this trip, he was going to let the last of his guard down and tell her how he felt about her. Being around her made him happier than he could ever remember being in his whole life.

But tonight wasn't the time to bring up the subject. He had work to do before he left in the morning. Maybe when he got back, they could have dinner, and he could take the time he needed to have a frank discussion with her.

"I'm leaving early in the morning. But Darcy?"

"Yes?" Her eyes searched his.

He took hold of her arms. "When I get back, I have something I want to talk to you about."

Her eyes widened. "You can't just go off and leave me hanging with those cryptic words. Tell me now."

He shook his head. "When I get back." He leaned in and kissed her cheek. "Good night."

She nodded. "All right. Have a good trip and be careful."

CHAPTER SEVENTEEN

Darcy replayed Ben's words in her mind over the next few days, hardly able to wait until he returned. What did he want to talk about? Surely nothing bad. The awkwardness between them had decreased, and they had slipped into an easy camaraderie—perhaps more than camaraderie if Darcy dared trust her instincts. And everything had been going great with the riding business. Plus, now they had Olivia.

While Ben was away, Darcy spent several hours with Olivia, teaching her the trails and acquainting her with how they operated. Olivia was a fast learner and a hard worker. After accompanying Darcy on several rides with customers, Darcy felt she was ready to start handling solo rides.

Darcy called Tim to ask him to update the website with more slots for bookings, and the slots instantly filled with clients. They'd also had inquiries about offering horseback riding lessons.

"I could teach riding lessons," Olivia told her, as they looked over the new schedule after the last trail ride. "The paddock is a perfect place."

"Are you sure you want to take on more

responsibility?" Darcy asked. "Because, like I told you from the start, I'm limited on how many hours I can put in out here."

"I'm sure. I have nothing but free time." Olivia's eyes sparkled at the prospect of doing more.

Darcy hugged her. "Olivia, you're an answer to prayer. I can't imagine how we thought we could handle everything ourselves, what with Ben and me being so busy."

"I can't thank you enough for giving me this chance. I love it here."

Darcy's phone chimed, and she glanced at the caller ID before answering. Although Josh had called a couple of times since the Sunday school outing, she had managed to avoid his calls. She didn't need him planting more ideas in her head about going home. The one night they had talked, a sense of homesickness had settled over her, and that was one feeling she didn't need. She had made a new life for herself in Wyoming, one she hoped would only get better over time.

Her heart did a little leap when she saw Ben's name on the caller ID. Swiping the answer button, she cried, "Ben! Are you on your way home?" Although he had called her while he was gone, he hadn't been sure when he would be heading back.

"I am. I should be back late this afternoon. And if you're free tonight, I'd like to take you to dinner."

She laughed. "That must mean you made a lot of money from your sales."

He chuckled with her. "I did okay. I can afford to take you out if it's not someplace too expensive."

"Anywhere is fine with me." As far as she was concerned, they could have made peanut butter and jelly sandwiches and taken them to the park. Just as long as she was with Ben.

"Great. How about I pick you up around seven?"

"I'll be ready. Drive safely and I'll see you then." She grinned as she pressed the end call button and stuck the phone back in her pocket. She looked up to see Olivia watching, her eyes dancing.

"So, you and Ben, huh?" she asked, a teasing smile playing about her lips.

Darcy couldn't help her widening grin in response to Olivia's observation. "Well, to be honest, no. But I'm hoping."

Olivia nodded. "I get it. It seemed like it took forever for my boyfriend to get the message I was interested in him."

Darcy glanced at her watch. "If you don't mind, I'm going to head back home and get ready."

"Of course. Have fun tonight."

"Thanks." With that, Darcy trotted back to her truck and waved goodbye.

"Wow, I didn't think you could look any more beautiful, but you proved me wrong." Ben's eyes traveled over her with a look of admiration.

Warmth flooded through Darcy's body. She knew she wasn't beautiful. Certainly not in the way Jolene was—or so she had heard. But she had taken special care to look her best tonight. She wore a flattering, bright yellow-flowered skirt and lacy white blouse that showed off her slim waistline, with strappy white sandals. She'd washed her hair and styled it in soft curls that framed her face and brushed her shoulders. Although she seldom wore makeup, she'd allowed herself some liberty with mascara and blush.

"Thanks. You look good, too."

Ben sported blue dress slacks with a beige shirt and a charcoal gray blazer.

She wanted to say how much she'd missed him but didn't want to appear too clingy.

"I've missed you," he said, pulling her into a hug, and making her laugh at herself for her hesitation.

"I've missed you, too," she admitted.

He released her and gestured toward the door. "Shall we?"

"Yes." She grabbed her denim jacket and her purse. "Where are we going?" she asked as they walked toward the truck.

"A little Italian place called 'Tony's.' It's not fancy, but the food is great."

"As long as it's not too expensive. I don't want you to blow all your money the first night."

He laughed. "As long as you don't eat too much, I'll be okay."

They talked about his trip and how great Olivia was doing and how they were looking to expand the business. Darcy barely noticed the ambience in the quaint little restaurant or the excellent food as her focus remained solely on Ben. How good it felt to be with him. In her happiness at seeing him and being with him, she temporarily forgot that he'd said he wanted to talk to her about something. Well, perhaps not *forgotten*, exactly, but she hadn't allowed any worrisome thoughts to spoil the evening.

An awkward pause ensued after the waiter cleared

away their plates. Finally, Ben took a long breath and reached across the table, grasping her hand. With his eyes intently on hers, he said, "Darcy, I want to ask you something."

Her heart skittered. "Yes?"

He lowered his eyes briefly before returning them to her face. Clearing his throat, he said, "I wanted to ask how you felt about me."

Wow. He's putting the ball in my *court. Why do* I *have to go first?*

She picked up her water glass to take a sip, but her trembling hand set it back down. Remembering how she had squelched her feelings after hearing Ben talk about Jolene, Darcy realized she had another chance. Swallowing hard, she said, "I like you a lot, Ben."

He nodded. "I like you a lot, too. But I wondered if . . ." He stopped and clamped his lips together for a moment while she willed him to continue. Finally, he said, "I wondered if you might consider me more than a friend."

"Yes, I do," she whispered so softly she wasn't sure if he heard her.

A broad smile lit up his face. "Then you would consider dating me?"

"Yes. I would love to date you." She felt a smile reaching across her cheeks, as well.

He released her hand and chuckled. "Phew. I'm sure glad *that's* out of the way." His tense facial muscles visibly relaxed. "Darcy, I'll be honest with you. I've been attracted to you for quite some time. But I didn't know how you would feel about being in a relationship with me. I don't have much to offer."

"What?" Her jaw dropped. "Not much to offer?

Ben, you are the nicest, most honest, hard-working man I know."

"You left out charming and handsome."

She laughed. "That, too. How can you say you don't have much to offer? What more could a woman want?"

A cloud passed over his features. "Well, materially, I don't have much. You know the ranch is struggling, although the sales from this week brought in some good money."

She tightened her lips. "Ben, wealth doesn't mean a thing to me. I hope you know that."

"Yes, but not many women want to be with a man who is constantly pinching pennies."

Darcy fixed him with an intense gaze. "Ben, I am not Jolene."

A look of surprise crossed his face before he replied. "I know that, Darcy. Believe me."

"So, we've got one more issue out of the way," she said lightly.

He didn't smile. "There is one other subject we need to bring out into the open."

Her brows drew together in a frown, and her heart skittered. "What?"

His eyes locked onto hers. "I know you were running away from something or someone when you left Pennsylvania. Would you tell me about it?"

Her shoulders sagged, and she sat back in her chair. "I suppose if we're taking the next step, I need to be honest with you." She'd not wanted to drag her baggage from Pennsylvania into her new life, but Ben deserved to know. She closed her eyes, debating on how to relay the ugly past, then decided to just spit it out.

"My fiancé, Josh, broke up with me a week before

our wedding."

Ben's eyes narrowed. "Ouch. Why?"

"The same old story. Another woman."

"A week before the wedding?" Ben said, his tone incredulous.

She nodded. "I didn't realize he was having misgivings. He never let on to me. As far as I knew, we were fine. But a coworker said something to him about the wedding getting closer, and he confided in this friend. The next thing I knew—or, actually *didn't* know at the time—his friend invited him out for a drink to talk after work. I never saw Josh drink, which is what made the whole thing so unreal. Anyway, while they were in this bar with Josh spilling his guts, another coworker, a woman named Zoe joined them."

With Zoe's name on her lips, Darcy heaved a disgusted sigh. "I'd met Zoe at some of Josh's advertising firm's social events. She came on way too strong around him. I always thought she had some nerve to openly flirt with my fiancé right in front of me, and I wondered how she behaved at work. But I didn't worry. I trusted Josh. We'd been together for three years, and he'd never given me reason to doubt his fidelity."

Ben shook his head. "I'm so sorry, Darcy. So how did they end up together?"

Darcy stared down at the table. "I don't know the exact details. All I know is a week before the wedding, Josh came to me saying he and Zoe were in love and he couldn't go through with the wedding." Tears sprang to her eyes, and she dabbed at them with her napkin. "We had everything lined up. The church, the minister, the flowers, the cake, the reception, the honeymoon. We had to call each of the guests and tell them the wedding was canceled. It was humiliating. We lost all our deposits, which was a lot of money for my parents." Her voice caught on a sob.

He took her hand once again and stroked the back of her hand with his thumb.

"I couldn't stay there. The whole town was talking."

"So, you ran away."

She raised her tear-filled eyes and looked at him. "I needed to go someplace where nobody knew about my past. I needed to start over."

"I understand. But let me ask you something else, Darcy."

She waited.

"Are you still in love with Josh?" he asked in a shaky voice.

Darcy shook her head. "No."

"You're sure? Because I don't want to be your rebound."

Her head whipped up. "Ben, no! I don't feel anything for him anymore. I'm in love with you!" She hadn't meant to spit those words out, but there they were.

He nodded, apparently satisfied. "And I'm in love with you, too." He squeezed her hand and let go.

She smiled through her tears and swiped at her face again with her napkin.

"To new beginnings," he said, raising his water glass to hers.

"To new beginnings."

CHAPTER EIGHTEEN

Darcy had always scoffed at people who said they'd found their soulmates, but now she understood what they meant. It was like she had found the other half of herself. She had to admit she'd never felt that way with Josh. Although Josh was attractive and intelligent, and they had a lot in common, her heart had never fluttered the way it did when she was with Ben. Even in the beginning.

She'd figured the lack of romantic thrill with Josh was just how real life worked. For her, the heart-throbbing, gut-clenching, dewy-eyed notion of love only existed in romance novels and chick flicks. Even when she thought Josh had shattered her heart, she wasn't sure if he truly had broken her heart or if she was merely reacting to being blindsided by his betrayal.

She sat in bed, her arms wrapped around her knees, and replayed the evening with Ben in its entirety. On the way home from the restaurant, the very air in the truck had been charged with the chemistry between them and the intoxicating smell of his cologne. The future stretched before them with new and wonderful adventures yet to be experienced. She looked forward to learning more about the complex man who sat beside her, his face shadowed in the darkness of the cab.

When they pulled up in front of her apartment, Ben shut off the engine and sat for a minute before turning to her. Finally, he said, "Since we're officially dating, would it be okay if I kissed you good night?"

Heat flooded over her, as her body responded with a longing of its own, and she turned her face toward him, unable to speak. He bent his head and gently brushed his lips against hers. Tingling surged through her veins at the feel of his soft, yet strong lips on hers. The kiss lasted only a brief moment but left her weak and breathless, her heart racing so quickly she feared she might faint.

She was glad for the opportunity to sit and compose herself while he hopped out of the truck and went around to open her door. As she slid from the seat, he put his arm around her and pulled her close for the short walk to her door. Then he lingered a moment before once more lowering his head and claiming her mouth with his. This time, he pressed more firmly, and she found herself kissing him back with an intensity that shocked her. She wrapped her arms around his neck, pressing her body into his.

Finally, he broke the kiss and stepped back. "Wow. You are amazing, Darcy Fuller."

She didn't trust herself to reply, as she stood trembling.

He grinned and said, "I'd better go. See you tomorrow?"

She nodded. "I'll be out after work." Her voice came out raspy.

He reached down one more time and gave her a quick peck on the lips, then turned to go. She watched him pull out and drive off, a sensation of missing him already rising in her chest. She walked into her apartment on rubbery legs and tossed her purse and jacket on the sofa. Then, unable to stop the adrenaline coursing through her body, she curled up in the middle of her bed, hugging her knees, thinking about Ben. Sleep would come with difficulty tonight.

Ben rolled the windows down and let the cool night air blow over him as he drove home. He needed cooling off after Darcy's passionate kiss. He should have known her kisses would be packed with as much passion as everything else in her life. How he could be so blessed to have a second chance at love, he didn't know. But then, as he thought about it, he honestly couldn't say he had been in love with Jolene. Infatuated, even in lust, but not love.

How he had mistaken those feelings for true love, he didn't know. But he knew now. Darcy had opened his eyes to what real love should be, and he hadn't even been looking. Quite the opposite. She had simply appeared in his life, and the sequence of events leading up to this night had been set in motion without his knowledge or consent. Maybe a higher power was at work. Not that Ben had prayed about finding love, but maybe God knew what Ben needed better than *he* did. Ben couldn't wait for their lives together to unfold.

The next day seemed to drag on, despite the

abundance of work that had piled up in Ben's absence. He stayed busy, his body on auto-pilot, while his mind counted the hours until he could see Darcy again.

"Boss, a little help here?" called Cam.

Ben looked up to see Cam trying to wrestle a rope halter on one of the steers for worming. The young beast wasn't having any of the restraint. Red-faced and sweating, Cam stopped and stood with his hands on his hips.

"Sorry," Ben muttered, moving along the steer's other side, as the animal bawled its distress. They managed to pin the animal between them, get the halter on, and the medication administered before the steer took off like a bullet.

Cam doubled over, his hands on his knees. "That one 'bout did me in." He ran his sleeve across his brow to wipe away the sweat. "Can I ask what's eatin' you today? Your head's not in the game."

"Guilty as charged. I guess I've been a little preoccupied." At Cam's sharp look, Ben added, "Just a lot of work to catch up on since being gone, that's all."

Cam's eyes continued to bore into Ben's. "Wouldn't have anything to do with that pretty lady vet that you couldn't stop talking about the whole trip, would it?"

Ben's lips tightened. "Of course not. Let's get back to work." He forced himself to put thoughts of Darcy aside as they rounded up the last of the young steers.

They finally finished the deworming and checking on the group of cattle that would be ready to take to auction in the next few weeks. The sun hung low in the sky, shooting pastel rays through the low white clouds, when Ben headed back to the barn, weary and grubby.

He dismounted from Kimber, turning him out into the paddock while he went to wash up in the outside sink.

Looking up, he saw Darcy's truck in its usual place under the live oak tree, but no sign of her. She must be out on a ride. He poked his head into the stable, but all the horses were accounted for. Perplexed, he dried his hands and face on the old towel that hung over the sink, noting that the towel was dirtier than he was. Maybe it was time to wash it.

"Ben!" Darcy's voice came from the back door of the house. She raced out into the yard and flung herself into his arms.

"Whoa, I'm sweaty and grimy." He disengaged her hold and took a step back.

"I don't care." She reached for him again, burying her face in his chest. "I've missed you all day."

A rumbling laugh erupted from his throat, as he stroked her messy ponytail with his less-than-clean hand. An image popped into his head of trying to give Jolene a spontaneous hug after working all day on the ranch, and her shrieking, "Eew! You're disgusting! Don't touch me until you've had a shower!"

He shook his head, trying to dislodge Jolene from his brain. He couldn't stand to have her constantly ricocheting around in his head when all he wanted to do was concentrate on the beautiful woman standing here hugging him, dirt, sweat, and all.

"I've missed you, too." He kissed the top of her head. "Cam called my attention to my *lack* of attention on the job today."

She looked up at him and grinned. "I hope I'm not a bad influence on you."

He grinned back. "You're a terrible influence.

You've totally corrupted me."

"Aha, I knew it!" came a voice behind them. They turned to see Cam leading his horse toward the stable. "You'd better watch that one, boss."

They both laughed and broke apart. "I've got to get four horses saddled up for a group that's due here in a few minutes," said Darcy.

"I'll help you," Ben volunteered.

"No. I can manage. Besides, as much as it pains me to say so, you really do need a shower. I don't object, but the horses might."

"Very funny. I'll get cleaned up. But how about dinner with me when you finish your ride?"

"It's a deal."

"You don't even know what I'm cooking."

"Doesn't matter." She shot him a huge smile before turning to go to the stable, and his heart turned to mush.

CHAPTER NINETEEN

"Ooh, somebody's holding hands," teased Molly, when Ben and Darcy walked into Sunday school.

Darcy's face flamed. She'd both looked forward to and dreaded the official "outing" of their relationship to their friends.

"Looks like it won't be long until they move into the young married class," said Kendra.

If Darcy's face had felt the heat before, she just knew that steam erupted from its surface now. She lowered her eyes, unable to speak.

"Hey, can I help it if Darcy has good taste in men?" said Ben.

"If that were the case, she would be with me," said Bill.

"Too late. I got to her first." The two men exchanged mischievous glances, as Ben tucked Darcy's hand firmly into the crook of his arm.

"I do hope you realize you've broken Molly's heart," said Kendra.

Molly's mouth dropped open, and for a moment, it seemed as if she couldn't find anything to say. But she found her voice. "Kendra, please let it go. Besides, you know I have a crush on Tim."

Tim's eyes widened and his face turned the color of an over-ripe tomato.

"Enough," said Audrey, who was filling in for the teacher. "It's time to turn our minds to spiritual matters."

Darcy didn't mind the teasing, as it further defined her and Ben as a couple. They soon settled into an easy rhythm, spending more time together and becoming completely comfortable with each other. She loved every aspect of ranch life, and often helped him in chores he would never have imagined a woman doing. He, in turn, listened to her talk about her days at the clinic and making her rounds to various farms, always expressing an interest and admiration in everything she did. Life couldn't have been more perfect.

It appeared the ranch had finally turned a corner financially. Ben had gotten a good profit from the sale of the steers, and the trail riding business was making more money than they would ever have imagined. Their tours remained booked, and Olivia had started up riding lessons, which had become popular.

One day Molly brought Tim out for another ride.

"I have to say I'm surprised to see you back, Tim." Darcy laughed. "I thought you never wanted to go near a horse again."

"I told him if he wanted to date me, he had to humor me in doing what I love," said Molly.

Darcy's eyebrows flew up. "You and Tim?" She glanced from one to the other.

"Yeah, I chased her until she caught me," said Tim, a shy grin on his face.

Molly rolled her eyes. "As if. I did everything but take out an ad on a billboard to get you to notice me."

"Molly, *everybody* notices you," Tim replied.

Darcy couldn't imagine a more unlikely couple—Tim, a self-proclaimed introverted nerd, and Molly, the outgoing, gregarious social butterfly. Maybe opposites really did attract.

"It's your fault," Molly told Darcy. "You and Ben set the example for the rest of us." Molly put her arm around Darcy's waist and started walking her away from Tim. "Excuse us a minute," she called over her shoulder. "Girl talk." When they had gone a few feet, Molly asked in a low, conspiratorial voice, "How is everything with you two? Spill."

Darcy beamed. "I've never been so happy in my life. Ben is wonderful. *Everything* is wonderful."

"Girl, you've got it bad. So, will we be hearing wedding bells soon?"

Darcy blew out an exasperated breath. "Don't be rushing ahead. We've only been dating a short time, and we're taking things slow. Remember, we've both been badly burned in the past." As their friendship had grown deeper, Darcy had shared about Josh with Molly.

"That was the past. You've both learned what a relationship with the wrong person looks like. But when you're with the right person, you know."

Darcy stopped and looked at Molly. "You really think Ben and I are right for each other?"

"Don't you?"

She nodded. "Yes, but I'm still a little scared."

"Why?"

"I don't know. Maybe I'm afraid of being too happy. I'm scared it will all be taken away from me."

Molly hugged her. "I wouldn't worry about that. I've known Ben for a long time. He would never hurt you."

"What if I hurt him? I wouldn't do so intentionally, of course, but sometimes things go wrong."

"Darcy, you can't tiptoe through life being afraid of all the 'what ifs.' I guarantee if you and Ben stay together, despite everything being peaches and cream now, difficult times will come. It's how you face challenges together that grow you as a couple."

Darcy's eyes twinkled. "How did you get to be so wise?"

"I've always been wise. Nobody takes me seriously, is all." Molly grinned at her. "I'd better get back to Tim before he bolts."

Darcy glanced over her shoulder. "We'd better get him on a horse before he changes his mind."

CHAPTER TWENTY

With Ben and Cam gone to another auction, Darcy tried to stay busy to keep her mind off Ben. She couldn't believe how much she could miss someone. She had never felt this way when she and Josh were separated for periods of time. Had she ever really loved Josh? They were compatible and comfortable together, but she couldn't remember ever having the giddy, head-over-heels feelings with Josh that made her stomach feel as though she were on a roller coaster. And his kisses never ignited the burning passion within the deepest parts of her being that Ben's did.

Looking back, she wondered how she could have allowed herself to settle for less. She supposed it was because she had never known any differently and assumed the intense emotions attributed to love were a fantasy produced by romance novels. If they had married, they would have probably been content, in a routine, boring kind of way, but she'd assumed that would be enough for a good marriage. She would never have known life could be so much better. She shuddered to think of what she would have missed.

Darcy tried to put Ben out of her immediate thoughts as she prepared for the last trail ride of the day. A weariness descended over her. She had done large animal calls all day until two. Then she'd come to the ranch and led two trail rides. After this last one, she had to hurry back to town and take calls for the weekend. She would be cutting it close. If Olivia weren't busy with lessons, she would have asked her to take this last group. She hoped Olivia could be persuaded to clean and put away the tack.

She had just finished getting the last horse ready when she heard a noisy pick-up truck barreling way too fast down the driveway, music blaring from the open windows. The driver slammed on his brakes, spewing gravel everywhere, and four rowdy teenage boys spilled out of the truck, laughing and jostling each other in fun. Mack raced over to the group, barking and trying to herd them into order.

Darcy frowned and marched over to the dirty white truck. "Excuse me, is this the Wilson party?"

"Hey, man, it's a party," said one of the youths, punching his friend in the arm. Mack continued his frenzied efforts to control the young men.

She raised her voice. "There's a speed limit posted on the entrance to the driveway. You can't just come storming in here like that. You'll frighten the animals."

One of the boys shot her a belligerent look. "Yeah, okay. Could you call off your dog?" He kicked out at Mack, but the agile dog easily avoided the blow.

Darcy put a hand on Mack's collar. "It's okay, boy, go on now." She gave the confused dog a gentle shove toward the house, then turned, her hands on her hips. "Look, this is a working ranch. If you're going to ride the horses, you will be expected to follow the rules. Otherwise, I'll have to ask you to leave."

"Hey, we paid a hundred bucks apiece to go riding," said one of the boys. "It's a birthday present for Brandon." He gestured with his chin to a tall, muscular boy next to him.

"Yeah," another boy chimed in. "It's Brandon's birthday, man."

"Come on, lady, we wanna ride. We'll do what you say."

Darcy regarded the group with rising annoyance and wondered if she should cancel the ride. But she didn't feel up to fighting a battle with these kids. They were probably just showing off and blowing off steam. She took a deep breath through her clenched jaw and blew it out slowly.

"I'll need you to fill out some paperwork." She turned to fetch her clipboard off the paddock gate.

"What kind of paperwork?"

"It's standard procedure," she said, flipping through the sheets to find the forms she wanted. "You are saying you promise to adhere to the rules of the facility and obey me, your leader. There will be no goofing around near the horses or while riding. You are also signing a statement that you will not hold the ranch responsible for any injuries that might incur."

The group exchanged amused glances. One of the boys made a crude comment and the others snickered.

Darcy gritted her teeth and passed out the papers. *Just let me get through the next forty-five minutes.*

After the boys signed the papers, she collected them and stuck them in the back of her clipboard. "Okay, follow me." She opened the gate to the paddock where five horses stood saddled and ready to go.

"Approach your horse quietly and slowly from the

left," she instructed the still-rambunctious young men. They settled down somewhat as she assigned horses and got the boys in the saddle, adjusted the stirrups, and showed them how to hold the reins.

After hoisting herself onto Windsong, she turned and said, "My name's Darcy and I'll be leading the trail ride today. You are to follow my instructions at all times. Form a single file line behind me. Stay in this line throughout the ride. Do not attempt to pass another horse. Do not allow your horse to get too close to the one in front. If your horse tries to veer off to eat grass, gently pull on one rein to move its head away from the grass. Do not make loud noises. When we get up on the ridge, stay clear of the cattle. Any questions?"

They all shook their heads. Darcy started off at a slow walk, constantly monitoring behind for any problems. After they had been riding for about fifteen minutes, one of the boys complained, "This is boring. Are we going to get to run?"

Darcy turned around. "Sorry. We only allow galloping for experienced riders. If you go through Olivia's riding class and she certifies you in more advanced techniques, then we can let you do more."

A couple of the boys groaned. "This is so lame, man."

"Our job is to keep you and the horses safe. The trail rides are meant to be taken at a leisurely pace."

"It's like the pony rides at the fair," grumbled another boy. "Where's the fun in that?"

"I'm sorry," she said, "but I thought you understood the conditions when you booked the ride."

The grumbling continued as they crested the ridge. They skirted around the cattle who grazed contentedly in the pasture, paying them little attention.

Suddenly, Brandon shouted, "Look at me! I'm a cowboy!" He jabbed his horse in the flanks with his heels and took off toward the herd. "Ye-haw! Get along cows!"

Laughter from the other three boys rang out behind Darcy.

"Brandon! Get away from the cattle!" yelled Darcy, turning her horse to follow him.

The startled cattle looked up and began to scatter, bawling with fear and kicking up clouds of dust and grass. Brandon rode into their midst shouting at the big, black beasts, and laughing as they ran, panicked, from him.

"Brandon, stop!" Darcy shouted, but her words were drowned out by the cacophony of bellowing cattle stampeding across the pasture.

A lone calf stood like a deer in the headlights as Brandon rode toward it, urging it to move. As Darcy caught up to Brandon, a massive cow came straight toward them. Her head rammed into Brandon's horse, causing both frightened horses to rear up. Darcy dug her heels in and held on as Windsong reared and then danced around the charging cow, whinnying her distress. Brandon flipped over backward and landed in the dirt, his left foot still caught in the stirrup.

The horrific scene before Darcy unfolded in slow motion. Brandon dangled from the stirrup while his horse continued to rear and the cow continued her attack. Darcy held her breath for fear Brandon would be trampled beneath one or enormous beasts. Brandon's screams could be heard as the thundering hooves crashed down again and again all around him. Darcy finally managed to urge Windsong closer to Brandon's panicked horse, where she grabbed the reins and pulled it away, dragging Brandon with them. The cow stopped and gave them one final warning look and a toss of her huge head before moving back toward her calf.

"My ankle!" screamed Brandon. "Get me out of this thing!"

Once they were safely away from the cow, and the horses had calmed down, Darcy dismounted and freed Brandon's foot. He let loose with a string of obscenities.

"My ankle's broke!" Brandon lay on the ground, covered with grass and dirt, angry abrasions discoloring both his arms and a large knot on the back of his head. Scrapes and bruises dotted his face, smeared by dirt and tears.

Too livid to speak, Darcy removed her backpack and fished out the first aid kit. She knew if she opened her mouth, she wouldn't close it again until she had berated the boy three ways from Sunday. But to do so now would serve no purpose. She pried open one and then the other of Brandon's tightly squeezed eyelids and examined his pupils. Normal and reactive. Good. She didn't know how hard he had hit his head, but a good-sized goose egg had formed on his skull in a short time. She placed her hand against his carotid artery, noting that although his pulse was high, it was steady and strong. Running her hands down his chest and abdomen, she found no tenderness. Then she turned her attention to his foot. Pulling off his shoe and sock and rolling up his jeans, she examined the ankle. Soft tissue swelling had already doubled the size of the joint, and bruising had crept in. Gingerly, she palpated the area.

Another barrage of obscenities assaulted her ears. She ignored them as she manipulated the foot to check for instability. Although swollen, she didn't detect any obvious fractures. However, a radiograph would be needed to confirm the extent of the damage. She ripped open an instant cold pack and wrapped it around the joint. Then she wound an Ace bandage over the pack and around the ankle in a figure-eight pattern. The scrapes and abrasions were minor and could wait.

She dug her cell phone out of her pocket and glanced at the bars, grateful for a signal. She punched in 9-1-1. When the dispatcher came on the line, she said, "This is Darcy Fuller at Whispering Winds Ranch, 344 Meadow Creek Lane. I need an ambulance as soon as possible for an injured horseback rider." She listened as the dispatcher asked a series of questions and she answered them to the best of her knowledge. "We are currently out on a trail, but I think we can safely transport him back to the house. Yes. Thank you."

Darcy ended the call and stuck her phone back in her pocket. Then she turned to the other three boys who had sat silent and motionless through the whole ordeal. "I need you to help me get Brandon on his horse. It will be faster to get him back to the house than to wait for EMS to reach us out here."

Their faces solemn and pale, the three dismounted and approached their friend who lay on the ground in the fetal position moaning and sobbing.

"Brandon, we need to get you back on your horse," she told the boy.

"Noooh," he wailed. "I can't move."

"We can get you help sooner if we can get you back to the house."

He swore at her again.

"Man, come on. We'll help you," said one of the others.

"Yeah, you got this, man."

They looked at her for instructions. "Okay, two of you get under his arms, and the other support his bad foot." As the boys worked together, she brought Brandon's horse close. "Brandon, we're going to help you up. All you have to do is hold on to the saddle horn. I'll lead your horse. Can you do that?"

"I'll try." He sounded more resigned to assisting in his own rescue.

"Good. Okay, guys, on count three, lift him up."

With all of them cooperating, they managed to get Brandon atop the horse. He gripped the saddle horn with trembling hands. Sweat beaded on his forehead and upper lip, and the color had leached out of his face. Darcy hoped he wouldn't pass out. "If you feel faint at all, let me know."

"I'm okay." The tough guy persona was starting to come back.

"Can you guys get back on your horses?"

They all nodded and turned to saddle up again. Although two of them struggled for a moment, they all managed to get astride their horses. Darcy climbed up on Windsong and took the reins of Brandon's horse, walking closely beside him. They rode back in silence, the trip seeming endless.

Once back at the house, Darcy dismounted and fetched a lounge chair from the porch on which to lay Brandon. With the help of his friends, they removed Brandon from the horse and got him into the chair. Olivia came running over.

"What happened?" Her wide eyes swept over the injured boy.

"A little accident," Darcy said through tight lips.

"Oh, my goodness! Is he okay?"

"I think so. But I've called for an ambulance."

Olivia fidgeted with nervous energy. "What can I do to help?"

Darcy massaged the back of her neck where a tension headache crawled up into the base of her skull. "If you could take care of the horses, that would really help."

"Of course." She turned to go when Darcy's cell phone rang.

Darcy pulled it from her pocket and groaned. "Oh no. I was on call as of six o'clock." She answered it and listened to the client patched through from the answering service.

"Yes. Yes. How bad is it?" She paused as the client described an injury to her dog. "Is it actively bleeding right now? Okay, good." Darcy closed her eyes and pinched the bridge of her nose. "It sounds like your dog is stable, but she will need stitches. I'm afraid I'm tied up with another emergency right now. I should be free in about an hour. Can I call you then and arrange to meet you at the clinic? Okay, thank you." She pressed the end call button and heaved a sigh.

"What's going on?" asked Olivia.

"It's a dog with a large cut that needs stitches."

"If you need to go, I can stay here and wait for the ambulance."

Darcy shook her head, exhaustion settling over her like a heavy, invisible cloak. "No, it can wait. I need to stay until the ambulance comes. This is my responsibility."

"All right, but I don't mind."

"Thanks. But if you'll take care of the horses, that will be plenty."

Olivia looked as if she wanted to argue further, but finally walked away to where the horses remained in the paddock.

They waited in silence, the only sounds coming from the chirping of the evening insects and Olivia untacking the horses. Darcy's spirits plummeted ever deeper with each minute that ticked by. At last, the shrill wailing of a siren broke the stillness, followed by the sight of the emergency vehicle's flashing red lights. Relief coursed through her as the ambulance pulled up the long driveway. Two paramedics hopped out, one carrying a medical bag.

They bent over Brandon and conducted a thorough examination while peppering Darcy and Brandon with questions. One of them unwrapped the Ace bandage and manipulated Brandon's ankle. He cried out but thankfully refrained from swearing.

"Looks like you did a good first aid job," remarked the older paramedic.

Darcy shot him a weak smile. "Do you think it's broken?"

"I think it's just a bad sprain, but we'll take him for an X-ray to be sure. He could have some torn ligaments."

The knot that had formed in Darcy's stomach grew into a fist.

As the paramedics prepared the gurney, a car turned in and raced up the driveway.

Brandon groaned. "Great. Who called my old

man?"

"I did," admitted one of the boys. "I thought he should know."

Brandon rolled his eyes.

Before the car had even stopped, the door flew open, and a tall, heavy-set man strode briskly across the yard. "What happened to my boy?" he growled.

"It's nothing, Dad," said Brandon. "Just a little accident."

"Accident? What kind of an accident?" He turned accusing eyes on Darcy. "Are you the one in charge here?"

"Yes, sir, I'm Darcy Fuller." She held out a tentative hand.

The man ignored it. "What kind of operation are you running here, anyway? How come you let my boy get hurt?"

Anger welled up in her chest, and her words spewed forth like erupting lava. "I didn't *let* him get hurt. He deliberately disobeyed instructions and put us all in a dangerous position."

"You're supposed to know what you're doing!" the man bellowed. He turned to the paramedics. "How bad is it?"

"We think it's just a bad sprain, but we're taking him to the hospital for an X-ray and to have the doctor look him over."

The man sputtered and his face turned an ugly shade of crimson, visible even in the dwindling light. Then he turned back to Darcy and jabbed a finger at her. "My boy's got a football scholarship to the University of Wyoming. If he's messed up his ankle because of your negligence, I'll sue your butt. Do you hear me? I'll *own* this ranch before I'm through!" His bulging eyes pierced hers.

Darcy's chest heaved with rage, but there was nothing she could say to this irrational man that would make any difference. She compressed her lips and willed her rapid heartbeat and respirations to slow.

The paramedics loaded Brandon into the ambulance, and the others got into their vehicles and followed without another word. Darcy closed her eyes, admonishing herself not to give in to the stinging tears threatening to overflow her bottom lids. Without even saying goodbye to Olivia, she grabbed her purse from the house and got into her truck. As she headed down the driveway, she called the client with the injured dog.

"It's Dr. Fuller," she said, trying to re-establish composure and professionalism. "I'm on my way to the clinic. I can meet you there in about twenty minutes."

"Oh, thank you, Dr. Fuller, but we got ahold of Dr. Tippins. He's taking care of Mocha as we speak."

Darcy's heart plunged into her stomach. They had called Dr. Tippins. He wouldn't be pleased. She drove as quickly as she could to the clinic, her stomach twisting. As she pulled into the parking lot, she could see all the lights on and two cars out front.

Gathering all her courage, she unlocked the back door and proceeded into the surgery room, where Dr. Tippins bent over a sedated chocolate Labrador. His head snapped up at her entrance.

"It's okay, Darcy, I've about finished up," he said. "What was the other call you were stuck with?"

Her chest constricted. He thought she'd been on a veterinary call, and for good reason. She'd given that impression to the client.

Her Adam's apple bobbed in her dry throat. "Actually, sir, it was a human emergency."

He raised his eyebrows, concern etched on his face.

She lowered her eyes and forced the words through her tight throat. "A rider fell off a horse during my last trail ride." No need to go into details.

Dr. Tippins' eyes hardened. "I see. Is the person okay?"

"I think so, sir. I had to call an ambulance."

He nodded. "All right. As I said, I'm almost done here. You can go on home."

She hesitated for a moment, then said, "Thank you, sir. I'm sorry you had to come in. Good night."

"Good night." He turned his attention back to his patient.

CHAPTER TWENTY-ONE

It had been a long day at the auction, and Ben probably should have stayed over another night. But he wanted to get back to the ranch. Back to Darcy. He missed her. He'd tried to call her twice from the road, but her phone went to voicemail. He couldn't remember if she was on call tonight, but he didn't want to disturb her if she was with an emergency. Thankful that Cam was driving, he laid his head back and dozed.

He was startled awake at the ringing of his phone. His heart beat a little faster at the prospect that it might be Darcy. Looking at the caller ID, a number he didn't recognize flashed on the screen. "Hello?"

"Ben, it's me."

His heart went into double time. He hadn't heard that voice for two years, but he'd never forget it. "Jolene?"

"Yeah."

Cam glanced over, his eyebrows raised. He mouthed, "Jolene?"

Ben gave Cam a curt nod.

A long pause followed on the other end of the phone. "Uh, Ben, I was wondering if I could see you. I need to talk to you about something."

His eyes narrowed, and he held the phone to his other ear, not wanting Cam to overhear any words that might leak through the speaker. "What do you want to talk about?"

"I'd rather talk to you in person."

Ben ran his hand over his face and shook his head. "Look, Jolene, I don't really—"

"Please, Ben, I'm in trouble."

He took in a ragged breath. "I'm sorry, but I don't know what I can—"

He could hear her crying on the other end of the phone. Blast it, why did she have to do that? He was always a sucker for a woman's tears. Ben blew a long breath of air out through his lips. "All right. Where are you?"

"I'm staying with Aunt Maudie for a couple of days. But I don't want to meet here. I don't want her to know. Can I come out to the ranch, maybe sometime tomorrow?"

A vision of Darcy danced across his mind's eye. No way did he want Jolene at the ranch. He didn't want to meet with her alone, and the last thing he wanted was for Darcy to run into her. "No, that's not a good idea." He paused, trying to think. It had to be a public place where Jolene couldn't cause a scene and he could make a quick exit if need be. "Um, I'm pretty busy tomorrow. I'm just getting back from an auction. How about I meet you Monday morning at the Coffee Shop in town around nine?"

She sniffled into the phone. "That's fine. Thank you. I'll see you then."

He disconnected the call before she could say anything else.

Cam glanced his way, a look of disbelief on his face. "Are you serious, boss? You're actually going to meet with that barracuda?"

Ben let out a long sigh. "She's in some kind of trouble, Cam."

"She *is* trouble! You don't want to go there again."

Ben frowned. "I'm not going there again. I happen to be in love with Darcy. I'm just going to see what Jolene wants to talk to me about."

Cam shook his head. "Whatever it is, you don't want to know."

"You're probably right about that," Ben muttered.

Ben finally crawled into bed around two a.m., his body dog-tired, but his mind running in circles. Why had Jolene reappeared after two years? And why was she coming to him with whatever problem she had? What did she expect him to do? He thought he'd seen the last of her. Why now, when his life was going so well? Whatever was going on with her, he'd listen, but that was all. He couldn't help her. He'd find a way to politely let her down and, hopefully, get rid of her.

He spent a restless night tossing and turning, not falling into a sound sleep until close to dawn. He'd planned on getting up early before church to take care of a few chores, but he slept through his alarm. A loud pounding on his front door jolted him out of a strange dream. Glancing at the clock, he wondered who would be banging on his door at nine o'clock on a Sunday morning. He quickly pulled on some jeans and a T-shirt and padded down the stairs in his bare feet.

A tall, heavy-set man wearing an angry scowl stood on his porch, his hand raised to bang on the door again.

Ben opened the door before the man's fist made contact.

"Yes, can I help you?" He rubbed sleep out of his eyes and ran his hand through his disheveled hair.

"Are you the owner of this place?"

"Yes. I'm Ben Parish. And you are . . ."

"Name's Paul Wilson. My son, Brandon, was injured by one of your horses yesterday."

"What?" Instantly awake, Ben felt the blood drain from his face. "How?"

"On one of your trail rides."

Ben stepped out onto the porch and sank onto a padded chair, his brain trying to process the man's words.

"Your trail guide is incompetent, Mr. Parish. She has no business being responsible for the safety of paying customers."

Ben's head was swimming. "Which guide?" Perhaps they had let Olivia take on rides by herself too soon.

The man pulled a cigar out of his front pocket but, thankfully, didn't light it. Ben's roiling stomach couldn't take the stench of cigar smoke. Paul Wilson stuck the cigar in his mouth and chewed on it. "I don't remember her name. Dark-haired girl."

"*Darcy*?" Ben's eyes widened.

"Yeah, I think that was her name," Paul said, his words garbled around the cigar. Removing the cigar from his mouth, he spat on the new floorboards of the porch. "My boy's ankle is busted up. Won't have the MRI until tomorrow to see how bad."

Ben struggled for words and found himself speechless.

Paul jabbed the cigar at Ben. "If my boy can't play football at State next fall because of the negligence of this place, I'm hiring me a lawyer. I'll sue you for everything you've got."

Cold fear paralyzed Ben's body. *A lawsuit*? How would he survive? He could lose everything.

"Just wanted to give you a heads up. If I were you, I'd fire that girl and shut down this operation. And get me a good lawyer."

Ben suddenly found his voice. He rose on shaky legs. "Now wait a minute, Mr. Wilson. There are two sides to every story. Let's get all the facts before we start talking lawyers. Maybe we can work something out."

Paul huffed. "You'd better pray my boy's okay, or I'll have your butt in court so fast your head will spin." He turned and stomped down the steps, the boards creaking in protest under his angry footfalls.

Ben flopped back on the chair, his whole body trembling. What on earth had happened yesterday? Darcy hadn't even called him. Why wouldn't she have called him about something so important? Was he in danger of losing his ranch? His initial panic gave way to fury. He needed to talk to Darcy, *now*.

Rising from the chair, he went into the house and took the stairs to his bedroom two at a time. He grabbed his phone from the dresser and checked to be sure she hadn't left a message. Nope, nothing. Flattening his lips, he punched in her number. The phone rang four times before voicemail picked up.

Saying a word under his breath that he rarely said,

he jabbed the end call button. He collapsed on the edge of the bed and put his head in his hands, trying to think. What was he going to do? His heart banged against his ribs so furiously, that he was afraid it might burst. He tried Darcy again. Still her voicemail. This time, he left a terse message. "Darcy, I need to talk to you as soon as possible."

Rising from the bed, he paced the length of the room, trying to collect his thoughts. He had planned to go to church, but now he just couldn't. Not in this frame of mind. There was no way he could smile and greet people and pretend his world hadn't just been shoved off its axis. Finally, he pulled on his boots and set out to work.

It was late afternoon before Darcy returned his call. By this time, he'd had several hours of mounting frustration and worry.

"Ben, I'm sorry I haven't had a chance to call. I've been on call all day and it's been one thing after another—"

"What the heck happened out here yesterday, Darcy?"

A short silence followed. "I'd hoped to talk to you before you found out."

"Well, how about right now?" His voice rose. "I've got some man threatening to sue me!" He plopped onto a hay bale, his free hand clenching into a fist and his jaw muscles tensing.

He listened as Darcy related the whole chain of events. Although his head told him it wasn't her fault, his body had been poised for a fight all day.

"Why didn't you call me last night?" he snapped.

"I . . . tried, but your phone went to voicemail. Then I got one emergency call after the other until it was so late, I didn't want to wake you."

He heard a catch in her voice, but his heart hardened.

"This is the first chance I've had all day to talk to you," she said, her tone soft and wounded.

Ben took several shallow breaths. "And what if this guy sues me?"

"Ben, the boy signed a waiver absolving us of liability. He's of legal age. And his injuries were the result of his own reckless actions and failure to comply with rules."

Ben huffed. "You know those waivers don't mean anything to an ambulance-chasing lawyer. They won't hold up in court. Legally, we're still responsible."

She didn't say anything for a minute. When she finally spoke, her words came out shaky. "If worse comes to worst, we have liability insurance. That's what it's there for. To protect us in situations like these."

He gritted his teeth. "And what if our insurance cap is less than what we are sued for?" Visions of his previous experience with insufficient insurance to cover losses sprang to the forefront of his mind. "Personal injury lawsuits can run into millions of dollars! I could lose everything!"

"Ben, I—"

"You shouldn't have let those kids ride. You said they were goofing around from the get-go."

"Ben—"

"It's *my* butt on the line, Darcy. I could lose the ranch my grandfather built." His chest heaved with anger.

"I'll call the insurance company first thing in the morning. I'm sorry." Her barely audible voice felt like a slap against the side of his head.

"*Sorry*?" He barked out a brittle laugh and shook his head. "I can't talk to you anymore right now." He ended the call and jammed his phone into his back pocket.

CHAPTER TWENTY-TWO

Ben's ugly words stung Darcy's heart. She understood why he would be upset and even angry, but his attack left her reeling. Would their fledgling relationship survive this blow? Her phone pinged with another call, and she had to tuck her whirling anxieties into a corner of her brain to deal with until later. How she wished she could have talked to Ben face-to-face, but this day with its constant onslaught of emergencies left her no time in which to do so. But she had never seen Ben so furious, and it scared her. She would just have to wait until he cooled off and pray they could work things out.

Darcy rose early after a mostly sleepless night. Not only was she exhausted from the unusually high number of calls she'd had yesterday, but she fretted as to how she and Ben would weather this storm. She had second-guessed herself ever since the accident, wondering if she should have canceled the ride and refunded the boys' money.

Dragging herself into the bathroom, she surveyed

her tired face in the mirror. Puffy, dark-ringed eyes stared back at her. How was she going to get through this day, physically and emotionally spent? She forced herself into the shower and let the hot water relieve some of the tenseness in her tight muscles. After dressing for work and taking a few sips of coffee, she counted the minutes until the insurance company opened. She spoke to a secretary who promised to have a claims adjuster return her call. With her stomach too tied up in knots to eat breakfast, Darcy headed to work.

Dr. Tippins called her into his office as soon as she stepped in the door. Her heart fluttered with dread. He was probably going to fuss at her for having to take her call Saturday evening. She trudged into his office, her heart in her throat, and waited for her reprimand.

"Darcy," he said, after closing the door behind her. "I've warned you repeatedly about your commitment to this practice. But Saturday night was the last straw."

A sick feeling filled her stomach. "I had to stay with the injured boy," she said, in a feeble attempt to defend herself. "I told the client I would handle the laceration when I was finished. It wasn't a life-or-death emergency."

"But it could have been." His voice raised a notch. "What if it had been an animal hit by a car or in respiratory distress?"

She lowered her eyes. He was right.

"I'm sorry, Darcy, but you seem to have made your choice. I'm afraid I'm going to have to let you go. Effective immediately."

Her head snapped up and tears pooled in her eyes. "Please, sir, it won't happen again." Her lower lip began to tremble.

"You can't make that promise. I have to look out for the welfare of my clients. I'm sorry. I've made arrangements for another veterinarian. He starts today."

A crushing numbness wrapped around her, and she didn't know how she would be able to put one foot in front of the other. In a daze, she left Dr. Tippins' office and made her way to her office where she collected her few personal belongings. Could these past couple of days get any worse? First the accident, then Ben's reaction, and now being fired. Hardly knowing what she was doing, she managed to make it to her truck, where she sat without moving. What was she supposed to do now? Her brain refused to form coherent thoughts.

Cars were pulling into the parking lot. She couldn't just sit here. Finally, she put the key into the ignition, started the engine, and pulled out, not knowing where to go. Her truck headed home, seemingly of its own volition.

But wait! Was that Ben's truck pulling into the Coffee Shop? If ever she needed to see Ben, it was now. Maybe since he'd had some time to calm down, she could talk to him. She needed his strength and his support right now. She'd never felt so lost. Slowing the truck, she watched as he exited his truck and strode toward the café.

She honked her horn and rolled her window down, yelling "Ben!" He apparently didn't hear her. Darcy turned her truck into the Coffee Shop parking lot, desperately searching for an open spot and finally finding one at the end of the lot. She dashed from her truck, yelling, "Ben!" as he opened the door to the café. The door closed before she could reach him. She paused for just a second, catching her breath, her hand on the door handle. Her eyes followed Ben's back as he made his way toward the rear of the restaurant.

Suddenly, a woman sitting at a table in the back jumped up and ran to him, throwing her arms around his neck and pulling his face down for a kiss. Darcy watched in stunned disbelief, her gut recoiling as if she'd been punched. Ben and the woman broke apart and the woman stepped back. Jolene! It had to be! A gorgeous, petite blonde wearing a form-fitting red sundress, she smiled up into Ben's face before grabbing his hand and leading him to her table.

Darcy stood gasping for breath, feeling as though someone had sucked all the oxygen out of the air. As she fought to stop hyperventilating, she became aware of a cascade of hot tears burning a path down her cheeks. Her knees gave way and she slumped to the sidewalk, burying her head against her knees. She didn't know how long she remained in her position, as time had completely stopped.

A couple exiting the café looked at her curiously.

"Honey, are you okay?" asked the woman.

Darcy took a hiccupping breath and nodded.

"Are you sure?"

"I'm fine." Darcy struggled to her feet and fled to her truck.

CHAPTER TWENTY-THREE

Ben stifled the urge to drag his sleeve across his lips to wipe away Jolene's kiss. Mortified at her public display, he knew tongues would soon be wagging. Maybe meeting her here hadn't been such a good idea. A park would have been better. He pulled his hand free from hers and took the seat opposite her at the table.

Wanting to waste no time, he said, "What did you want to see me about?"

She flashed her sweetest smile, the one that had ensnared him when he'd been too naïve to see through her. It wasn't going to work today.

"Thank you for coming, Ben. I knew I could count on you."

He waited.

"Gosh, you look good." Her cornflower-blue eyes roamed over him.

A waitress Ben knew appeared at their table, raised an eyebrow, then asked, "What'll you have?"

"Just coffee," he said, wishing he was anywhere but here.

"Oh, Benji, don't you want breakfast? I'm starved." Jolene batted her long lashes.

He cringed at the name she used to call him. "Then

order something, Jolene. I'm not hungry."

Jolene sighed and closed the menu. "I'll have the special."

The waitress hovered until he repeated, "Just coffee."

When she finally went away, he said, "Tell me what's going on, Jolene. I don't have all day."

Her smile evaporated and her flirtatious eyes filled with tears. "I'm pregnant, Benji."

His eyes traveled to her ringless left hand. "Congratulations," he said in a flat tone.

"No. You don't understand. I can't stay with Liam. He . . . he's abusive. I'm leaving him."

Ben frowned. Despite everything she'd put him through, Jolene didn't deserve an abusive partner. "I'm sorry. What can I do?"

She nibbled on her quivering lower lip. "I was wondering if I could have my engagement ring back. I need money to get away." Her voice lowered. "And an abortion."

He felt as though she'd struck him. "Jolene, no."

"I can't raise a kid. I've got no place to live, no job . . ." Her voice trailed off. "I don't want Aunt Maudie to know."

Don't let her get to you. Ben sighed and looked away. "I'm sorry, but I don't have the ring. I had to sell it to pay the mortgage on the ranch."

Jolene hung her head. The tears flowed in earnest now.

"Look, I can give you a few hundred dollars. I did well at the auction. There's a crisis pregnancy center in Jackson Hole. They can help you. Get you a place to live, a job, help with expenses."

She shook her head. "I don't know."

Ben fished out his wallet and laid five hundred dollars on the table. "Please, Jolene. If you have an abortion, you will always regret it. If you don't feel you can raise a child, you can place the baby for adoption. Lots of people are desperate to adopt newborns."

Jolene wiped her face with a napkin and looked up at him, tears shimmering in her eyes. "I'm sorry for messing everything up, Benji. Nobody was ever nice to me the way you were."

He squeezed her hand. "It'll be okay."

"What kind of family emergency?" Ben asked, worry constricting his chest. Olivia had flagged him down the minute he pulled up to the house.

"Darcy didn't say," Olivia told him. "She just said she had to fly back to Pennsylvania this afternoon."

Ben's stomach churned. He ran a hand across his face, feeling terrible for how he had spoken to her yesterday. Is that why she'd called Olivia instead of him? He needed to apologize. "Did she say how long she would be gone?"

"No, just that she had to leave immediately."

He pulled his phone from his pocket and tapped her number. Straight to voicemail. With a hesitant voice, he said, "Darcy, I'm sorry about yesterday. Please call me. I need to know you're okay."

CHAPTER TWENTY-FOUR

Darcy buried her face in Marigold's neck, relishing the honest smell of horse. "I've missed you, girl. I was going to take you back to Wyoming with me, but we're better off here. This is home."

Darcy had risen at dawn and made her way to the stable, the one place on earth where she felt she belonged. She'd tried to pray, but she couldn't find words. Besides, God knew how broken she was. The last couple of days had been a nightmare, even worse than when Josh had betrayed her. She'd never imagined Ben could be so cruel and hypocritical.

How long had he been seeing Jolene behind her back? The image of them kissing would be permanently seared in her brain. Still, although she felt dead inside, it was better that she find out now, before investing more time and emotions in a relationship that had no chance of going anywhere. So why did she mourn the loss of something she'd never had in the first place?

"Honey?"

Darcy raised her head from the comfort of her faithful horse. At least *someone* was faithful. Mom stood behind her holding a tumbler of coffee.

"I thought you might need this."

Darcy smiled and reached for the tumbler. "Thanks, Mom." Mom always knew how to make her feel better. After pouring out her soul to her parents last night, they had given her the space she needed.

Mom stroked her back. "I'm so sorry things didn't work out in Wyoming."

Darcy swallowed back tears and nodded. "It just wasn't meant to be."

"Don't get me wrong. I'm thrilled you're home, but I hate to see my girl hurting."

Darcy took a faltering breath. "I'll be okay. I'm home now."

"It's been a week, and she hasn't returned my calls," Ben complained to Francine. "I'm really worried about her. I know I messed up. Big time."

He was grateful to Francine for not agreeing with him. She changed the subject. "Did you hear from the insurance company?"

Ben nodded. "Just this morning. Their lawyer subpoenaed the hospital report on Brandon. He suffered a bad sprain, but no fractures or torn ligaments."

"Well, that's good news."

"Yes, praise God. He should be fine in a couple of weeks. Plus, they talked to the other boys. They all confirmed Brandon was completely at fault."

"Have you heard any more from Brandon's father?"

"No, but our lawyer believes he'll drop the threat of a lawsuit, as he doesn't have much to gain."

"That's even better news."

Ben sighed. "None of what happened was Darcy's

fault. But I was so shaken up by the idea of a lawsuit that I took all my fears out on her. And now she won't talk to me."

Francine squeezed his hand. "Have any of her other friends heard from her?"

"She hasn't returned any of their calls, either."

"It sounds like you have a lot of praying to do. I'll pray, too."

"Ben, Kimber's been lame on his left foreleg for a couple of days," said Olivia. "I can't find anything obvious, but we might need to get Dr. Tippins out to have a look."

Ben's jaw tightened. If it wasn't one thing, it was another.

"I wish Darcy were here. She could look at it." Ben closed his eyes, the weight of the world pressing in on him. He missed Darcy so much he ached, and with every day that went by without hearing from her, he feared he had lost her for good. He couldn't stand the thought that he had finally found the one woman he wanted to spend the rest of his life with, and he had driven her away.

At first, he figured she truly was tied up with a family situation. But her continued failure to return his calls made him heartsick. It was becoming painfully obvious that she didn't want to talk with him. But why? He'd apologized for being angry and lashing out at her. She had every right to be hurt. But was she *that* unforgiving?

He sighed. "I'll look at Kimber. If I don't see

anything, I'll give the doc a call."

After examining the horse, Ben said, "I think he might be developing a sole abscess. His foot is warm, and he seems tender on the back part of his hoof." He pulled out his phone and punched in the number for Doc Tippins.

"Hi, Pam, it's Ben Parrish. I was wondering if I could get Doc Tippins out to look at one of my horses. I think he may have a sole abscess."

"Dr. Tippins is out of town for the weekend, but I can have Dr. Spencer come out."

Ben frowned. "Who's Dr. Spencer?"

"He's Dr. Tippins' new associate. He took Darcy's place."

Ben's heart began thumping in an erratic cadence. "What do you mean he took Darcy's place? You mean he's filling in while she's gone?"

"No." Pam lowered her voice. "I thought you knew."

"Knew what?" Tendrils of fear crawled up his spine.

Pam's voice softened even more to the point where he had to strain to hear. "I thought she would have told you." She sighed. "Look, I'm not supposed to know what transpired, but talk gets around. Darcy was fired for not being available during an emergency."

"What? When?" Even as he asked, he had a pretty good idea, and his gut twisted.

"That night the boy got hurt on the trail ride. She was supposed to be on call, but she was delayed getting to the clinic while she waited for the ambulance. Dr. Tippins had to cover for her."

Ben's heart threatened to stop altogether.

Everything that had happened during that terrible weekend flashed through his mind. First the accident, then him blaming her, and finally, her getting fired. No wonder she didn't want to talk to anybody. He should have been there for her. Instead, he had heaped more pain on her.

At his silence, Pam asked, "Did you want Dr. Spencer to come out?"

"What?" He couldn't think straight. "Oh, yeah. Thanks, Pam."

"He can be out there around two."

"That's fine." Ben disconnected the call and stared out into space.

"What's wrong?" asked Olivia.

Ben suddenly seemed to realize she was still standing there. "Did you know Darcy was fired from her job?"

Olivia's eyes widened. "No! She didn't say anything to me. Just that there was a family emergency."

Ben was starting to doubt the emergency had anything to do with Darcy's family. The emergency was Darcy, herself. She had felt hopeless and abandoned, and she had run again. Back to where she felt safe. And it was largely because of him. If he could only talk to her, tell her how much he loved her. At least she hadn't blocked his number. But she didn't respond to his messages, either. How he wanted to hold her in his arms and make all the hurt go away, especially the hurt he had caused.

CHAPTER TWENTY-FIVE

It felt so good to be home. Darcy spent hours riding Marigold along all the familiar trails, places where she had grown up and felt safe. This was where she belonged. Running away to Wyoming had been foolish. Slowly, her frozen heart began to thaw as she allowed the peace and security of everything she loved to surround her.

For two weeks, she'd done nothing but eat, sleep, pray, and ride Marigold. Her parents had been there whenever she needed them, but they didn't hover. Her tired body began to regain strength, and her battered soul found comfort in simply letting go. At some point, she would have to start looking for a job, and she would love to work for her parents again, but right now she cherished life in the moment. When thoughts of Ben popped into her mind, she refused to allow herself to dwell on them, banishing them to the archived memories section in her brain. If only her heart got the message.

Darcy finished brushing Marigold's bronze coat and settled on the soft grass, closing her eyes to enjoy the warm sunshine.

"Darcy?" called Mom. "There's someone here to

see you.”

Darcy hadn’t heard her mom approach. Shading her eyes with her hand against the glare of the sun, she looked up. Someone to see her? Who? She hadn’t contacted any of her old friends since being home. She’d been happily cloistered away from the world where no one could hurt her. But her parents had probably talked, so word had gotten around.

“Who is it?”

Mom hesitated. “It’s Josh.”

Josh! Her heart skipped a beat. He was the last person she wanted to see. Well, maybe the next-to-the-last person, Ben being the last. She jumped to her feet. “I don’t want to—”

“Darcy!” Too late. Josh was already halfway across the yard, a huge grin on his face.

“I’m sorry,” said Mom. “I told him to wait.”

Darcy sighed. “It’s okay. I had to run into him sooner or later.” She walked the rest of the way to bridge the gap between them. They stood facing each other, neither saying anything.

Finally, Josh took a step closer and gave her an awkward hug. Releasing her, he said, “I’ve missed you, Dar. But I’m not here to put any pressure on you. I just want us to be friends again. Do you think we could do that?”

The bitterness she’d harbored for so long toward him dissipated as she slowly nodded. What was the point of staying angry? She really didn’t want things to be strained between them. They both had to live in this small town.

“Let’s take a walk,” she said.

They strolled side-by-side in silence toward the

large pasture where several horses grazed. Darcy tried to untangle the jumble of feelings fighting for her attention. Josh had hurt her deeply, but she knew he regretted his actions. He probably hurt as much, if not more, than she did, knowing he'd caused such pain and thrown away their future together. Still, she wasn't about to open her heart again. To anyone. She didn't know how many times a heart could break and still go on beating.

They settled on a wrought-iron bench warmed by the sun, outside the fence and gazed at the horses for several minutes. Josh leaned forward, resting his elbows on his knees, his eyes still focused on the pasture.

"I'm glad you're back, Dar."

This time, she didn't bother to correct his pet name for her. For some reason, it didn't annoy her like it did when she had talked to him on the phone. In fact, it felt rather familiar and comfortable.

"I'm sorry things didn't work out in Wyoming for you, but I'm not sorry you're home." He fidgeted, clasping and unclasping his fingers. "I can only say again how sorry I am for what I did."

Darcy nodded. "I know."

He took a hesitant breath. "You're still the only woman I've ever loved. We had a good thing going until I let Zoe mess with my head."

Darcy grimaced at Zoe's name. She didn't want to ask, but she had to know. "Is Zoe still at the firm?"

He shook his head. "No. Things were too awkward after we broke up. She took a job in Pittsburgh."

Darcy twisted her body toward him. "And why *did* you break up?"

"Because we were never right to begin with. I knew that from the start. She wasn't you." His eyes sought hers.

Darcy's throat tightened. If she weren't careful, she could allow herself to be caught up in the familiar and comfortable. If nothing else, she and Josh had a history that had mostly worked well until Zoe. But she couldn't define what she felt for him now.

"You said you wouldn't pressure me."

He grinned. "I'll try not to. But it won't be easy."

Against her will, she grinned back.

CHAPTER TWENTY-SIX

Although Ben didn't feel like being around people, he let himself be talked into going out to lunch with his Sunday school group after church. Maybe if he forced himself to get out more instead of holing up at the ranch, he'd feel better. They took seats at the large round table in the center of Francine's, and for once, Ben was glad Molly sat next to him. With her nonstop talking, he wouldn't have to listen to his own thoughts.

After the requisite amount of small talk, Molly asked point blank, "So, have you heard anything from Darcy?"

So much for a distraction from his thoughts. Ben shook his head. "No, and I don't think after all this time I'm going to."

"I've tried calling, too, but she won't return my calls, either." Molly reached over and laid her hand atop Ben's. "I don't understand it. Why would she just disappear without a word to any of us?"

The others, all ears tuned in to the conversation, agreed the situation seemed strange. Ben had shared with them how he had blamed Darcy for the accident at the ranch and how awful he had talked to her. But none of them thought that was reason enough for Darcy to simply disappear without a word to anyone but Olivia.

"Maybe she was embarrassed at having been fired," said Kendra. "Losing your job is a major blow to a person's ego."

"She could have easily gotten another job," argued Molly. "Maybe one where she wouldn't have had to take call so much."

Ben nursed his iced tea so he wouldn't have to participate in the conversation he didn't want to have. The job loss might have been the final blow, but he knew if he hadn't upset Darcy so badly, she would have just sucked up the loss and moved on, just like Molly said. Darcy loved working at the ranch. And he thought she loved being with him—that is until he turned all Jekyll and Hyde on her. How he wished he could go back and relive that day, take back the way he'd berated her. She'd felt badly enough about the accident. He should have had her back, not thrown her under the bus. He ached with wanting to hold her again and make up for the horrible words he'd said.

"It was because of me, okay?" Ben snapped. "*I'm* the reason she left."

They all stared at him and then glanced at each other as if afraid to further stir the hornet's nest. He excused himself to go to the restroom. When he came back, the talk had moved to other topics, although everyone still seemed to walk on eggshells around him. The food arrived, and as Francine set down plates, she patted his shoulder. The lunch was subdued, and everyone but Tim and Molly left as soon as they had finished eating, rather than lingering around the table fellowshipping.

Ben stood to go, as well, but Molly placed a hand

on his arm. "Ben, wait."

He sat back down, feeling rotten for ruining everyone's good time.

"Stop blaming yourself. We all say things we regret when we're upset. You've tried to apologize. That's all you can do."

"I miss her, Molly," he said, his voice trembling. "I want her back."

"I know. I wish there was some way to get her to talk to us."

"She has to come back sometime," said Tim. "All her stuff is still here."

Ben brightened. "That's right. She flew to Pennsylvania. She'll have to come back. Maybe I can get her to talk to me then."

"If we know she's back," said Molly, throwing a damper on his poorly thought-out plan. "We can't exactly stake out her apartment indefinitely."

"True." He slumped in his seat.

Molly squeezed his hand. "Don't give up. I'm going to keep calling her until she either gets sick of seeing my number and answers the phone, or blocks my number."

Despite himself, Ben grinned. Molly was as tenacious as a dog with a bone. If anyone could get through to Darcy, Molly could.

Darcy galloped Marigold around the perimeter of the property, her hair loose and flying behind her, hoping the ride would clear her head. Thoughts of Josh's visit a few days ago nagged at her. Since the day he'd shown up at the stable, he had kept his distance. For that, she was grateful. But sooner or later, she would have to deal with what to do about him.

He had made his intentions clear, despite his claim to the contrary. He wanted her back and he was willing to wait for her to come around. Darcy tried to dissect through the swirling confusion in her brain. Everything had happened too fast. She still hadn't processed the sequence of events that made her flee Wyoming, and now she had to deal with how she felt about Josh.

As her mother pointed out, Josh was a good man who had made a mistake. A big mistake. But before the Zoe fiasco, as Darcy had come to regard that dreadful incident, she and Josh had always gotten along well, rarely arguing. They had similar tastes and enjoyed most of the same activities. Her parents liked him. Josh had a strong work ethic and did well at his job. He'd always been polite, attentive, and supportive. Plus, his good looks turned heads. So what if his kisses didn't trigger fireworks or his touch send shivers of excitement through her body? Those mountain-top passions weren't sustainable over time. People had to live in the real world.

She could do worse than Josh, right? Then why did melancholy grip her heart when she envisioned a life with him? It was Ben's fault. He had opened her eyes to what love could be, even though she knew it could never be with him. Jolene had captured his heart, and he'd never really gotten it back. Was there someone else out there who could stir Darcy's blood like Ben had? Someone who could make her heart do flip-flops and her stomach swarm with butterflies? But she didn't want to start over looking for Mr. Right when Mr. Good

Enough stood within reach. Maybe good enough was all anyone really needed.

Her phone buzzed, forcing her out of her reverie. She plucked it from her pocket and looked at the caller ID. Molly again. Darcy sighed. She felt guilty for evading her Wyoming friends these past few weeks. After all, they hadn't been the ones who hurt her, and she was being just as hurtful by refusing to talk to them. Besides, she owed them an explanation.

She swiped the receive call button. "Hi, Molly."

An infectious laugh reached her ear. "Well, you *are* still alive! We've all been wondering if you were abducted by aliens."

Darcy grinned. Her heart swelled with affection for this woman who had taken her under her wing from the beginning. "No, nothing like that. I'm sorry I haven't returned your calls, Molly. I wasn't up to talking to anyone. It was rude of me."

"Hey, I'm just glad you're okay. You *are* okay, aren't you?"

Darcy thought about the question for a second. "Yeah, I'm getting there. Thank you for your concern. It means a lot to me."

"I'm so sorry for everything that happened to you, Darcy. None of it was your fault."

"I'll admit I wished that little black cloud hovering over me would move on." Darcy changed the subject. "So, how have you been? And Tim? And Kendra and everyone?" She deliberately did not ask about Ben, but she knew Molly wouldn't be fooled.

"Tim and Kendra and I are fine. Ben, not so much."

Darcy had to bite her tongue, but she refused to be drawn in by Molly's reference to Ben.

"You'll be glad to know the Wilsons have not pursued the lawsuit. Brandon's ankle is okay. He just had a bad sprain."

"That's a relief." Darcy hated leaving Ben to deal with the aftermath of the accident, but she'd had no choice.

"The other boys confirmed that Brandon disregarded rules and caused the accident. You couldn't have prevented anything."

"Good. I'm glad." A load of worry and guilt lifted from her shoulders. Despite what Ben had done, she didn't wish for him to become entangled in a lawsuit that could potentially threaten his ranch.

Molly paused. "Darcy, Ben is beating himself up over blaming you."

Darcy's pulse spiked. She knew Molly would get around to the subject of Ben, which is why she'd put off talking to her for so long. "It's understandable. He had every right to be upset."

"But he's kicking himself for taking his anger out on you. Then, when he found out you'd been fired on top of everything else, he . . . Darcy, can I ask you something?"

Darcy hesitated. "What?" she asked, her tone wary.

"Are you coming back to Wyoming?"

Darcy sighed. "No, I'm not."

She heard Molly catch her breath. "But why? You can easily get another job and . . . and Ben needs you. He's lost without you."

Darcy huffed out a bitter laugh. "Ben needs me? Where's Jolene?"

"Jolene?" Confusion laced Molly's voice. "What does she have to do with anything? She's been gone for over two years."

To her dismay, Darcy realized tears sluiced a path down her cheeks. "That's what you think. That's what *I* thought until I saw Ben kissing her in the Coffee Shop." Darcy's voice caught on a sob.

"Jolene?" Molly's voice rose in disbelief. "Darcy, you must be mistaken. When? When did you see them?"

Darcy hiccupped. "The morning I got fired. I was driving home and saw Ben's truck turn into the Coffee Shop. I followed him. I needed him so badly at that moment." Her words rushed out intermixed with her tears. "But when I reached the door to the café, I saw him and this beautiful blonde wrapped together in a passionate lip-lock."

"I can't believe it."

"That's why I'm not coming back to Wyoming, Molly. There's nothing left for me there."

Molly didn't say anything for a long minute. Finally, she said, "Look, Darcy, I don't know what you saw, but I can assure you Ben is not with Jolene. He's devastated over losing you."

Darcy wiped her sleeve across her face. "He's not the man I thought he was, Molly."

"Oh, Darcy. That's not true. He . . ." She stopped, and Darcy heard a sharp intake of breath. "I'm going to get to the bottom of this. I want to find out the truth just as much as you do. But please, don't make a final decision about coming back until I talk to him."

"I won't promise. He lied and cheated."

Molly sighed. "All right. But would you promise me something else?"

Darcy took a ragged breath. "I don't know."

"Promise me you'll take my calls. I miss you."

Darcy sniffled and nodded, although Molly obviously couldn't see her. She swallowed around the lump in her throat. "Okay. I miss you, too."

CHAPTER TWENTY-SEVEN

"What were you thinking seeing Jolene again, let alone kissing her in public?" Molly laid into Ben the minute he opened his door. She barged past him into the kitchen, where she whirled on him, her fiery dark eyes spearing him with angry darts.

"What?" Ben stepped back, momentarily stunned. Then he ran a hand across his face. "Oh. The small-town gossip mill. I should have known word would get out."

Molly planted her hands on her hips, her nostrils flared. "Well?"

Ben had never seen Molly so furious. He sank into a kitchen chair. "Have a seat."

"I'll stand, thank you."

Tempted to laugh at her righteous indignation, he quickly stifled the urge and assumed a more appropriate facial expression. Nothing about this situation was funny.

"She called me out of the blue and said she was in trouble. She begged me to meet her. I didn't want her coming out here, so I told her to meet me in the Coffee Shop. Probably not the best idea."

Molly continued to glare at him. "Neither was

kissing her.”

Ben’s lips flattened. “I didn’t kiss her. She kissed *me*.”

“Semantics.” Molly crossed her arms over her chest and leaned against the kitchen counter.

“No, it’s not.” His skin crawled at the idea he would willingly kiss Jolene. “Believe me, I didn’t want to be anywhere near her.”

Molly raised her eyebrows. “Yet there you were. Why?”

Why indeed? His eyes drifted to the ceiling, searching for an answer. “Because I’m a nice guy, and when someone tells me they’re in trouble, I can’t walk away.”

She moved over to the table, pulled out a chair, and sat. Her tone softened. “So, what kind of trouble is Jolene in?”

He met Molly’s eyes briefly before lowering them to the table. “I’m not at liberty to share Jolene’s problems. I gave her some money and some advice, and that’s the last I saw of her.”

Molly snorted. “You better hope that’s the last. If she knows she can squeeze money out of you, she’ll probably keep turning up like a stray cat.”

He sighed. “I told her I couldn’t do any more for her, that she was on her own after that day. And that’s it. I haven’t seen or heard from her since. End of story.”

Molly’s eyes sought his. “Except it’s not the end of the story.”

Ben’s brows furrowed. “What do you mean?”

Molly blew out a long breath. “Darcy saw you.”

He felt the blood leach from his face, and his heart stuttered. “What? How?”

"She was driving past the Coffee Shop right after getting fired. She saw your truck and needed your shoulder to cry on. Only your shoulder was occupied."

Ben closed his eyes and leaned his head back against the chair. A moan escaped from his lips.

"That's why she went back to Pennsylvania. Not because you blamed her for the accident, but because she saw you kissing Jolene."

His stomach recoiled. No wonder Darcy wouldn't talk to him. She thought he had betrayed her just like Josh. His poor, beautiful Darcy. What must she be feeling toward him?

He opened his eyes, blinking away tears. "What am I going to do, Molly? How can I explain?"

She shook her head. "I don't know. Darcy's pretty upset. I'm not sure you can fix this."

"I have to try." He reached across the table and gripped her arm. "Molly, you've got to help me. If she won't talk to me, will you talk to her for me?" He let go of every shred of pride, his voice breaking. "Please. You've got to make her understand."

Molly looked him in the eye again. "I'll talk to her. But, Ben, she says she's not coming back here."

Ben sat at the table after Molly left, his head in his hands. "Lord," he whispered, "show me what to do. I don't want to lose her." Tears streamed down his face. "I know you brought us together for a reason, Lord. Please heal her heart and let her know I would never betray her."

No answer came from heaven. He sat waiting,

unaware of time passing until Olivia knocked on the door. He couldn't let her see him like this.

He went to the door but didn't open it. "Yes?"

"I just wanted to let you know Dr. Spencer is here to recheck Kimber's hoof."

Ben blew out a frustrated breath. Was there no rest for the weary? Ever since Darcy had left, his mind hadn't been on his job. Everything felt meaningless and empty.

"I'll be there in a minute." He rose and went to the kitchen sink where he splashed cold water on his face.

Olivia eyed him when he stepped out the door. "Are you okay?"

"Yeah." He pulled his Stetson lower to shield his face and cleared his throat. "I think I'm coming down with a cold or something."

CHAPTER TWENTY-EIGHT

Darcy finally felt strong enough to venture outside of her imposed isolation at home. Mom had talked her into going out to lunch in town, and Darcy had to admit that getting out had lifted her spirits. She ran into several old friends and enjoyed catching up. Nobody seemed to be looking at her with pity and nobody brought up the mortifying past.

As they were leaving, Darcy's phone chimed. Josh. Her heart stuttered a little. She still hadn't come to any decision, and she realized he had been more than patient.

Mom glanced over at the caller ID. "Are you going to answer?"

Darcy hesitated, then swiped the answer call. "Hi, Josh."

"Hey, Dar. MacKenzie just called and told me she saw you at Peco's Grill."

Darcy laughed. "News sure travels fast in small towns. Mom and I just finished lunch."

"That's good. I'm glad you're getting out." He paused. "Uh, Dar, if you don't need to get home right away, there's a horse show going on at the fairgrounds."

"Yeah, Mom mentioned something about that."

Mom mouthed, "What?"

Darcy covered the phone with her hand and said, "The horse show."

Mom nodded.

"I was thinking maybe you'd like to head over with me and check it out."

"Now? Aren't you at work?"

He chuckled. "It's Saturday. Have you lost track of the days?"

Had she? Her head had been in such a fog these past few weeks. Darcy shot a look at her mother, who smiled and said, "Go."

"Okay."

"Great. I'll swing by Peco's and pick you up in five minutes."

Darcy and Josh climbed up onto the metal bleachers and took seats warmed by the sun. Dressage had just begun, and Darcy lost herself in the beauty of the competition. Although she had never competed in dressage, she had always admired the art. Watching the horses and riders infused her with a sense of peace, and her immediate surroundings faded away as she became engrossed in the beauty of the demonstrations.

She had almost forgotten Josh's presence beside her until he reached over and took her hand. Her heart jumped, and an involuntary gasp slipped through her lips. In the ensuing few seconds, her mind see-sawed between snatching her hand away or leaving it where it rested. But her hand felt warm and pleasant in his.

Turning to him, she gave him a shy smile. He beamed back at her and snuggled closer. She allowed herself to be content in his easy company.

After the last competition, they made their way through the crowd to the fairground exit and to the parking lot, still holding hands.

As they reached the car, he turned to her, his expression taking on the look of a hopeful puppy. "How about dinner?"

She bit her lip, then nodded.

They ate a casual dinner at a popular café in town, where a stream of people continually stopped by their table to welcome Darcy home. No one seemed surprised to see them together. Darcy basked in the easiness of being back where she belonged.

Josh took his time driving her home. Although they hadn't talked much throughout the day, there had been no awkwardness between them. They pulled up to her door, but Josh made no effort to get out of the car.

"Thank you for going out with me, Dar," he said, shifting his body toward her, his face reflected in the light of the full moon. "I had a great time."

"Me, too," she said, realizing she meant it.

His hand brushed against her cheek. "May I kiss you goodnight?"

Darcy swallowed, her heart suddenly picking up pace. She raised her face to his, and he brushed her lips gently with his. Then, putting his arm around her shoulder, he pulled her closer and deepened the kiss.

She waited for the tingles of excitement, but other than the agreeable sensation of his mouth against hers, no sparks ignited. A fleeting image of Ben's face flashed through her mind, and a tinge of disappointment settled over her.

Josh released her and opened his door, coming around to walk her to the house. Standing in the glow of the porch light, he said, "I love you, Dar." He gave her another soft kiss before leaving her standing there, more confused than ever.

CHAPTER TWENTY-NINE

Since their outing to the horse show, Josh and Darcy had been spending a lot more time together. They fell into an easy routine, hardly seeming as if they had been separated for the last several months. Although thoughts of the episode with Zoe still had the potential to rear its ugly head at odd moments, Darcy tried to let it go. She couldn't change the past and she had to think of the future.

Her phone buzzed a couple of times while they watched a movie at the local theatre, but she swiped it off. Now, back in her room, she pulled the phone from her purse and checked the voicemail.

"Hi, it's Molly. I really need to talk to you. Call me back. It's important."

Darcy debated for a minute as to whether or not to return the call. Her life was starting to get back on track, and she didn't want Molly trying to derail it. But she'd promised she wouldn't avoid Molly again. Darcy glanced at the clock. Wyoming was two hours behind, so it wasn't too late to call. She thumbed through her contact list and hit Molly's number, a little hope springing in the back of her mind that Molly wouldn't answer.

Molly picked up on the first ring. "Darcy. Thanks for calling me back."

"Sure. What's up?" Darcy sprawled on her bed, tucking an arm under her head.

"I talked to Ben about Jolene."

Darcy closed her eyes and tried not to sigh. She didn't want to go down the "Ben" road again. It was too late.

"Darcy, they are *not* back together. He met her that one time because she called and begged him to. She said she was in trouble. He talked to her for a few minutes and that was all. She hasn't been back since."

Darcy didn't respond. So what? Ben obviously still had feelings for Jolene.

"Are you still there?"

She gritted her teeth and said, "Yes, but it really doesn't matter."

Molly's voice rose. "Yes, it does! He's in love with you, Darcy. He is miserable without you."

Against her will, Darcy blurted out, "What about them kissing?" Why did she even care anymore?

"Darcy, Jolene kissed *him*. He didn't encourage her. He only met with her because he's the kind of guy who can't stand to see someone in trouble."

A crushing tiredness weighed on Darcy. She just wanted to go to sleep and never wake up again.

"Did you hear me?"

"I did, but—"

"Please give him another chance."

Another chance. Another chance. Why did everybody want her to give them another chance? *Because God gave you chance after chance.* Great. Now she had God's grace to remind her of her unforgiving spirit, making her feel worse.

Darcy stood and walked to the window, staring at the darkness outside. "Thanks for telling me, Molly. I'm sorry for misjudging Ben and jumping to the wrong conclusion. But I'm still not coming back." She took a hesitant breath. "Josh and I are back together."

"Darcy, no!"

"I'm flying out to Wyoming next week to clean out my apartment and get my truck. I'll call you when I get there and maybe we can have lunch or something."

"Would you at least consider seeing Ben?" Molly pleaded.

Why did Darcy's heart suddenly hurt? "I . . . I don't think that would be a good idea."

Molly's voice rose in indignation. "Darcy, you owe him that much. At least have the decency to face him and say goodbye."

"I'll think about it. Bye, Molly." Darcy disconnected before Molly could nag her anymore and heaved a weary sigh. She tipped her head up to look at the shimmering stars and the nearly full moon shining in the black sky.

"God," she whispered. She couldn't formulate coherent words to utter anything else. The scripture about the Holy Spirit interceding for us when we don't know what to pray sprang to her mind. She sure hoped He was praying for her. She'd never felt so adrift.

CHAPTER THIRTY

Darcy inserted her key into the lock of her Wyoming apartment. Mixed feelings assaulted her. On one hand, she felt just as much at home here as in Pennsylvania. On the other, she felt like an intruder who didn't belong. She'd refused her mother's and Josh's offers to come with her to help her pack and drive back. She needed the time alone to think—for all the good *that* was doing her. Her thoughts had only chased themselves in circles around her brain.

The weather had grown chilly since she'd left, and she shivered as the wind whipped against her thin jacket. The knob finally turned, and the door opened into her stuffy apartment. She wanted to throw open the windows to get some fresh air flowing through the rooms which had been closed up, but the apartment was already cold and the outside temperature colder. Shrugging, she cranked up the thermostat and opened the windows. So what if the electric bill sky-rocketed? She wouldn't be here that long. She didn't have much stuff to pack from the furnished apartment.

Darcy opened the storage room, glad she hadn't thrown out the packing boxes from when she'd moved in. Pulling the boxes into the living area, she began to pack her books and her few personal odds and ends. With the first box full, she hunted for the packing tape, finally locating it in the desk drawer in her bedroom. She smoothed down the top of the box and stretched out a generous amount of tape, which curled and stuck to itself in a tangled mess. Frustrated, she wadded it up and started over.

Her doorbell sounded. Good! That must be Molly. She could help with this recalcitrant tape.

"Molly, you're early," she said, throwing the door open wide. Only it wasn't Molly. Ben stood fingering the brim of his hat in his hands. The wind blew his longish, dark hair into his face. Dark stubble sprouted on his chin and cheeks. His intense blue eyes locked onto hers.

Darcy's breath caught, and her heart began flopping around in her chest like a fish. She couldn't force words past the tightness in her throat, so she stepped back, her rubbery legs failing to support her.

He reached out and caught her, his cold hands against her skin sending fingers of fire up her arms. Ben grinned, making her even dizzier. "I guess I should have asked if I could come in, but it seemed expedient for me to do so."

She still couldn't find her voice as she gazed into those eyes. How had she forgotten those mesmerizing eyes in such a short amount of time?

Ben released her and looked around. "You're packing," he said, his teasing tone suddenly going flat. The smile disappeared from his face.

Darcy nodded. "I'm . . . going home." She settled onto the box she'd just filled.

He ran a hand through his windblown hair, his eyes

imploring her. "Darcy, please. I'm so sorry for everything that happened. But I want you here. I need you here."

She shook her head, tears welling up in her eyes. "I can't."

Ben crossed the short space between them, knelt, and gripped her arms again. "Why not?"

Darcy lowered her eyes, tears dripping onto her shirt. "My life is back in Pennsylvania. I never really belonged here."

"Yes, you did! You do!" His fingers dug into her arms. "Don't leave me, please! I love you, Darcy."

The tears flowed faster. "Don't make this harder for me, Ben." Her words came out muddled through her tears.

"Darcy, look at me." He tilted her resistant chin up. "I love you. Can you honestly say you don't love me?"

She shook her head. "It's too late."

He stood and pulled her body against his, crushing her against his chest and laying his head atop hers. "It's not. Please. Give me another chance. Stay for a few days. Then if you still want to leave, I won't stand in your way."

"I can't." She wanted so badly to just stay in his arms, but she had made her decision. It was time to stop wishing things had been different and get on with her life. Josh was waiting for her. Her parents were waiting for her. Her new job at Caryville Animal Hospital was waiting for her. So why couldn't she move? Her racking sobs soaked into Ben's flannel shirt, and he began stroking her back, his light touch igniting sparks along her spine. If she didn't step away from this man quickly, she would be lost forever.

"I've . . . I've got to go home. Please, just leave, Ben." She wrenched herself from his arms and fled to her bedroom, closing the door.

Ben stood staring at Darcy's closed door, his heart splintering into tiny pieces. What more could he do? Should he go after her and demand she open the door? Should he continue to beg? If he kissed her senseless, would she relent and stay? Or would she only become angry?

He might as well face it. He had lost her. Replaying the events that had led up to this moment, he knew he only had himself to blame. Unbidden tears sprung to his eyes. Crossing the short expanse of space to her bedroom door, he hesitated for a moment before knocking.

"Darcy? I'm going. I just want you to know I love you. I will always love you. If you change your mind, call me. I'll always be here for you."

No answer came from the other side of the door. He scrubbed a hand over his face, then let out a weary breath. Placing his hat on his head, he walked out of the apartment, shutting the door softly behind him.

Devoid of all feeling, he got into his truck and started the engine, his mind completely closed down. On autopilot, he drove slowly through the main street of town, barely registering everyone and everything around him. Suddenly the phone on the seat next to him chirped.

Darcy! Ben reached for the phone, his shaking fingers fumbling it, knocking it to the floor. Taking his eyes off the road, he bent down to retrieve it. The last thing he remembered was the thundering sound of metal against metal and a tremendous impact into the side of his truck, flipping him over and over before everything went black.

CHAPTER THIRTY-ONE

Darcy didn't know how long she lay sobbing on her bed after Ben left. She must have fallen asleep, for the ringing of her phone startled her awake. She sat up, rubbed her grainy eyes, and reached for the phone. Molly. She wasn't up to talking to Molly, let alone seeing her today, as they had planned. She almost let voicemail pick up, but then afraid that Molly would just show up at the apartment, Darcy answered.

"Darcy! It's Ben!" Molly shrieked into her ear before she had even said hello.

The fog clouding Darcy's brain blurred Molly's words.

"Darcy! Are you there?"

Darcy massaged her aching forehead and said through her thick throat, "Yes. I . . . fell asleep."

The sound of hysterical sobbing came through the phone. "Ben's been in an accident!"

Darcy's heart froze. The fog evaporated, her mind now on full alert. "When? What happened? Is he hurt? Where is he?" The questions spilled out of her mouth before Molly could respond. Darcy glanced at her watch, realizing it had been over an hour since Ben left her apartment.

In faltering words, Molly said, "Another truck hit him broadside and rolled his truck. They've taken him to the hospital."

"How badly is he hurt?" Fear clamped Darcy's gut, and in that moment, she knew without a doubt that she loved Ben with all her heart and couldn't lose him. How had she so foolishly let him walk out that door? How had she let her confusion blind her to what stood right in front of her?

"They don't know yet. He's unconscious."

Darcy took shallow breaths, trying not to panic and failing. What if he died? "Molly, I have to see him. Will you drive me to the hospital? I don't think I can drive."

Molly's agitated voice rose. "I can't. I came upon the accident while they were loading him into the ambulance. I'm shaking all over. Tim's on his way. We'll pick you up." She hung up.

It's my fault. The condemning words repeated over and over in Darcy's mind. Despite the furnace pumping warmth into the over-heated room, Darcy felt chilled to her soul and couldn't stop trembling. She clasped her shaking hands together in an effort to stop the shivering and willed her teeth to stop chattering. Trying to block out the mantra playing in her head, she closed her eyes and whispered, "Please, God. Please, God." The continuing entreaty temporarily drowned out the accusing loop running through her brain.

A soft knock sounded at her door, and belatedly Darcy realized she looked a mess with her swollen red eyes, tear-stained cheeks, and uncombed hair. But it didn't matter. She raced to the door and fell into Molly's arms, both of them sobbing. Tim stood behind Molly, shifting from one foot to the other.

Through garbled words, Darcy spilled her heart to her friends about how she was to blame for the accident.

"It was an accident," said Tim. "Blaming yourself won't help. Come on. Let's get to the hospital."

Calm and in control, Tim escorted the distraught women to the car and drove to the trauma center in Jackson Hole. Darcy managed to regain some composure by the time they walked through the doors of the emergency room.

They approached the nurse behind the desk. "Excuse me," said Tim, "we're here to check on a man brought in from a truck accident. His name is Benjamin Parish."

The nurse looked up and squinted at them over the top of her glasses. "Are you family?"

The group glanced at each other before Tim said, "No, ma'am, his only family is a brother in Denver. I've called him, but he won't be here for a few hours."

Darcy's heart sat like a weight in her chest. The nurse wasn't going to let her see Ben. She *had* to see him. To tell him she loved him. If he died . . . She squeezed her eyes shut to block out the thought. But whatever happened, Ben had to know she loved him.

The nurse wavered for a moment before saying, "The doctor is in with him now. I'll have him talk to you when he's finished, if you'll take a seat." She gestured to the large waiting room filled with people.

The three shuffled to hard plastic chairs lining the wall. As they sank into the seats, Tim said, "We need to pray."

Darcy and Molly nodded, and they all gripped hands.

Tim began. "Father, we thank you for your blessings and your mercies, and we know You are always in control. We ask you, God, to heal our brother, Ben. We don't know the extent of his injuries, but You do. We pray You reach down and touch him. Restore him to us. Guide the hands of the doctors and nurses attending him. Let Ben feel Your presence, peace, and comfort. We ask this in the name of Your Son, Jesus Christ. Amen."

Molly went next. When she finished, all Darcy could add was, "We love him, Lord. *I* love him. Please don't take him from us."

They sat in silence for what seemed like an eternity until the doctor finally appeared. He motioned for them to follow him to a corner of the room where they could have more privacy.

The doctor got straight to the point. "Your friend has a severe concussion and is still unconscious. He doesn't appear to have any internal injuries, which is encouraging, but we'll have to watch him closely for the next forty-eight hours to be sure nothing unexpected pops up. We're moving him to ICU for monitoring."

"When will he wake up?" Darcy asked.

The doctor shook his head. "We don't have any way of knowing."

"But he *will* wake up?" she persisted.

"I'm sorry. I can't tell you that either. We'll have to wait and see."

Darcy bit her lip to keep from screaming. He *had* to wake up.

"Can we see him?" asked Molly.

"Once he's settled in the ICU, you can visit for fifteen minutes, one at a time."

They moved to the ICU waiting room and sat for another eternity before a nurse came to get them.

"I want to warn you. He's pretty banged up," she said. "He has a lot of bruising and swelling on his face and chest from the airbag deploying, and abrasions from the seat belt digging into his shoulder. But those two things probably saved his life." She looked at the anxious trio. "Who wants to come in first?"

"You go, Darcy," said Molly, giving her a little push.

Darcy hesitated a moment, then taking a deep breath, she followed the nurse into the restricted area, her boots echoing loudly on the polished tile floor, sounding loud and out of place in this hushed environment. With her heart fluttering in fear, she tried to mentally prepare herself to see Ben.

The nurse led her to a cubicle near the central nurses' station and pulled back the curtain. Darcy gasped. If she hadn't known the man lying in the bed was Ben, she would never have recognized him. Black-and-blue discolorations surrounded his swollen eyes, and angry red marks and bruises marked his face. His bare chest also sported bruises, and a diagonal abrasion from his left shoulder to his waist marred his flesh. His lips were cracked and swollen.

Several wires attached to his contused chest led to a monitor next to the bed which displayed his heartbeat in a hypnotic sequence. Darcy held her breath and watched the ECG for signs of arrhythmia, but to her relief, the steady beeping confirmed a regular rhythm. Tearing her eyes from the monitor, she forced them to travel over the rest of Ben's body. A Foley urinary catheter led from under the sheet to a plastic bag hung on the bottom of the bed. An IV line attached to a pump dripped saline at a steady rate into his left arm. A blood pressure cuff on his muscled right arm periodically squeezed and released, recording the results on the monitor. A pulse oximeter hung on his right index finger, its red glow shining through the skin. A large bandage wrapped around his forehead to the back of his head.

Darcy sank into the chair next to the bed and took Ben's ice-cold hand. Closing her eyes, she clasped it between her own hands, willing her warmth into his body. Tears trickled down her cheeks and onto his hand. She wiped them away with her sleeve.

"Ben," she said, her voice catching. "I love you. I've been so stupid, not knowing what I wanted or where I belonged. I'm sorry it took this accident for my eyes to be opened. If you'll wake up and come back to me, I swear I'll never doubt again. I know God brought us together for a reason. I can't believe He would take you from me now." She sniffled and looked around for a tissue on his nightstand. Plucking a tissue from the box, she let go of his hand and blew her nose. Then she grasped his hand again, bringing it to her lips and kissing it.

"Miss, I'm sorry, but your time is up," said the nurse, pulling the curtain aside.

So soon? Darcy had just gotten here. She couldn't leave him yet. What if something happened and she wasn't here? But she knew Tim and Molly were waiting for their turns.

She nodded and slowly got to her feet. Before going, she leaned over and whispered into his ear. "I love you, Ben. Please come back to me." She kissed his cold, unresponsive lips, then followed the nurse to the ICU door, looking back over her shoulder. What if this was the last glimpse she would ever have of him?

Darcy spent the next two days and nights curled up on the vinyl couch in the ICU waiting room, visiting Ben as much as the hospital protocol allowed. The entire Sunday school class, as well as other friends and Dave, came and went. Apparently, Molly had not enlightened anyone else about Darcy's intention to move back to Pennsylvania.

"We're so glad you're home," said Kendra, drawing Darcy into a bear hug. "We've all missed you."

"Is everything okay with your family? We heard there was an emergency," said Audrey.

Fingers of guilt gripped Darcy for allowing the deception to continue. But at the same time, she was relieved she didn't have to explain. At this point, she couldn't sort out her own feelings, let alone explain them to someone else. All she knew was she loved Ben, and that was all she could handle right now. Everything else—Josh, her family and friends in Pennsylvania, and the job she was supposed to start—blurred into eddies of confusion in her head.

Not trusting herself to speak, she simply nodded.

Dave took her hand. "You're the best medicine Ben could have. If anyone can pull him out of this, it's you."

Darcy swallowed around the lump in her throat. If only they knew she was responsible for Ben's condition. They would never forgive her.

Around midnight, she sat alone in the dimly lit

waiting room. At night, normal hospital sounds quieted. No announcements for doctors blared over the intercom. The footsteps of the nurses were less hurried and softer, and voices muted. She glanced at her watch. The ICU nurse should be summoning her soon for her few-minute visit. Ah, here she came.

"Any change?" she asked when the nurse appeared.

"Not yet," the woman said.

Darcy's expectations fell as she followed the nurse into the now familiar area. She braced herself for the helplessness she always experienced when the hours ticked by with no change in Ben's condition. Settling into the hard chair beside him, she took his hand, as she had so many times over the past few hours.

"I love you, Ben," she said again, for perhaps the thousandth time. "Please forgive me. Please come back to me." She sighed, as the hope within her began to ebb away.

Wait! Did he just squeeze her hand? Her heart jumped into her throat. Did she really feel something or was it just her imagination?

"Ben," she said, her voice more urgent. "Can you hear me? Squeeze my hand if you can hear me."

She waited, adrenaline pumping through her veins. Yes! A definite pressure. Loathe to let go of his hand, she laid it gently on his chest and hopped up to call the nurse.

"He squeezed my hand!" Her voice rose in excitement, and she reminded herself to speak more quietly, as several critically ill patients occupied the ward.

The nurse hurried over. "Mr. Parish? Ben?" She shook his shoulder, then opened his eyelids to examine his pupils. As she raised his second lid, he grimaced and opened his eyes.

"He's awake!" cried Darcy in a harsh whisper. She maneuvered between the nurse and the bed as Ben blinked several times. She smoothed back the dark hair along his forehead, as his eyes focused on his surroundings.

He coughed and stretched his shoulders. "Wh . . ." he croaked.

Tears streamed down Darcy's face. "Oh, praise God! I thought I'd lost you."

The nurse explained what had happened as Ben struggled to sit up, confusion on his face. Then she left to notify the doctor.

Ben turned to Darcy, the purple bruising around his eyes fading into yellow. But his blue eyes were clear as he gazed at her. "I thought I'd lost you, too," he murmured.

CHAPTER THIRTY-TWO
(Six months later)

"I don't know what I could possibly have been thinking," Darcy said as Molly zipped up her tulle and lace ball gown wedding dress, with a fitted bodice and a full skirt.

"I'm thinking you're both a couple of horse fanatics, so getting married on horseback only seems natural. It beats getting married while skydiving."

"Yeah, it seemed like a good idea at the time." Darcy turned to examine herself in the full-length mirror. "But how I'm going to get on a horse in this dress is beyond me."

Molly laughed. "You and everyone else." She held out her own full skirt of pale pink satin.

Darcy's mom opened the door and stepped into the room, her eyes shining as she appraised Darcy in her wedding dress. "You look like a dream." Her mom crossed the room and wrapped Darcy in a hug. "I'm so happy for you, honey. You've made the right choice."

"Thanks, Mom." Her parents had been more supportive than she could ever have imagined.

Her mother stepped back and held Darcy at arm's length. "This is a beautiful place. You belong here. And you belong with Ben."

Joy welled up in Darcy's heart. She didn't know why it had taken nearly losing Ben to realize where she belonged. Ben recovered quickly from his injuries, amazing the doctors. But Darcy knew the Great Healer had performed the true miracle. After seeing Ben's totaled truck, she knew the hand of God alone had not only saved Ben's life but had prevented major injuries. He'd been back to work on the ranch within a few days of the accident.

Darcy had taken a part-time job with a multi-doctor veterinary practice, one in which she didn't have to be on call so often. She spent all her spare time at the ranch, building up the trail riding and riding lessons business, as well as doing minor redecorating of the ranch house. She didn't want to make major changes to Ben's childhood home, just enough to establish her own presence.

Her dad poked his nose into the room. "Are you ready, Princess?" Then he let out a whistle. "Wow. You look beautiful, sweetheart."

"Thanks, Daddy." She moved toward him, her full skirt rustling across the wooden floor. She reached her arms around his waist and rested her head against his strong chest, inhaling the outdoorsy scent of the cologne he had worn since she was a little girl. How blessed she was.

"Let's get this show on the road," said Molly, breaking the bittersweet moment. "If Tim has to sit on that horse for much longer, he's going to have a meltdown."

They all laughed and headed to the paddock, where saddled horses waited to take them to the meadow. Ben and Darcy had chosen that location because, in the spring, the meadow came alive with a stunning display of wildflowers.

Olivia, Kendra, Audrey, and Molly led off with Darcy's mom. With Dad's help, Darcy settled atop Marigold. Darcy's full skirt billowed out behind her in the warm breeze as they slowly made their way to the meadow.

When they rounded the trees, Darcy got her first glimpse of Ben astride Malachi, and her breath caught. Dressed in a black tuxedo, his dark hair blowing gently around his face, he'd never looked so handsome.

The bridesmaids rode forward, one by one, and brought their horses to a stop at the side of the minister, who had firmly refused to conduct the ceremony from the back of a horse. He stood eyeing the massive beasts on either side of him and took a couple of steps back.

It was time. Darcy and her father rode side-by-side up the grassy aisle between the few guests who stood in the soft sunshine. Her eyes locked onto Ben's as they moved forward, everything so perfect it seemed unreal.

Ben watched in awe as his beautiful bride made her way toward him. A fleeting thought of the contrast between now and the first time he'd seen her coming toward him in her baggy brown coveralls ran through his mind, and he grinned. Only God could have designed a woman so perfect for him. And only God could have orchestrated the events to make sure they ended up together, despite the circumstances that had threatened to drive them apart.

As if in a dream, they spoke their vows, and the next thing Ben knew, the minister was pronouncing them husband and wife. Ben dismounted from Malachi and climbed up behind Darcy on Marigold, pulling his new bride back for a long kiss. Hoots and cheers rang out from the small crowd. Then, a huge smile stretching across his cheeks, he turned Marigold around and spurred her into a walk back down the grassy aisle.

As they rode through the small group of spectators, Tim yelled, "Can I get off this horse now?"

Ben laughed and said, "I don't think we'll ever make a horseman out of Tim."

"I don't want to talk about Tim," Darcy replied, as she settled into his arms.

"What *do* you want to talk about, Mrs. Parish?"

Her mischievous eyes twinkled. "I don't want to talk at all," she said, as she tipped her head back for another kiss.

THANK YOU, DEAR READER

If you enjoyed reading this book, the best thing you can do to help the author is to tell others about it. Ellen would also greatly appreciate you rating her book and leaving a brief review at amazon.com and goodreads.com. Simply type in the name of the book and the author. When the website comes up, click on the picture of the book, scroll down, and there will be a button to click to leave a rating and a review. A review doesn't have to be long—a sentence or two telling what you liked about the book. Was it interesting, humorous, informative, thought-provoking, etc.? Thank you so much for your support.

Ellen would love for you to visit her website: https://ellenfannonauthor.com and subscribe to follow her weekly blog, *Good for a Laugh.*
Follow Ellen on Facebook: ellenfannonauthor

Award-winning author, Ellen Fannon, is a retired veterinarian, former missionary, and church pianist/organist. She and her retired Air Force pilot-turned-pastor husband have fostered more than forty children, and have two adopted sons. She has published six novels, and her stories have appeared in *One Christian Voice, Chicken Soup for the Soul, Divine Moments, and Guideposts; and her devotions have appeared in Open Windows, Guideposts God's Creatures, and The Secret Place.*

Please visit Ellen's website, *Good For a Laugh*, and sign up to follow her weekly blog at: ellenfannonauthor.com

WATCH FOR BOOK TWO IN THE LOVE IN THE WIND SERIES, *FALLING FOR A COWBOY* TO BE RELEASED SOON
CHAPTER ONE

Always a bridesmaid, never a bride. The unwelcome thought popped into Kendra Clark's head without warning as she pulled into the long driveway leading to Whispering Winds Ranch, one of the most beautiful places in southern Wyoming. Now where had *that* thought come from? Oh, she knew where. The last time she had been here she had been a bridesmaid in Ben and Darcy's wedding. Ben Parish, the owner of

Whispering Winds had fallen hard for Darcy, the pretty new veterinarian who had moved to Wyoming to start a new life after her fiancé had dumped her a week before their wedding. Not so different from Kendra's own experience with her high school sweetheart, Aaron. Everyone, including them, expected them to get married, even though they had gone their separate ways to college with the understanding they would get married when they graduated. But the distance and time apart had pretty much killed their relationship. Well, that and the fact that apparently, Aaron hadn't considered remaining true to her during their four years apart a necessity. While she had been faithfully waiting for graduation when they could finally plan their wedding, he had been enjoying the company of numerous other coeds.

Although Kendra had been angry and disappointed, what bothered her most was the many opportunities she had passed up to date nice young men who had expressed an interest in her. Meanwhile, Aaron, too cowardly to admit the truth, had continued to lead her on, letting her think he was as anxious to start their life together as she was. Four wasted years later, he confessed he wasn't ready to settle down. By then, Kendra realized she had been more in love with the idea rather than the reality of Aaron. She'd never really known him at all.

Bittersweet memories of Ben and Darcy's fairy-tale-like wedding filled her mind as her tires crunched along the pebbled driveway. Not that she wasn't happy for them—she was. But it seemed like everyone in her singles' Sunday school class had paired up, leaving her the odd man out. Or, to be more accurate, the odd woman out. At the rate things were going, at the ripe old age of thirty-two, she'd be the only one left in the singles' class at church. Maybe she should promote herself to the old ladies' class. She felt more and more like an old maid as she watched all her friends get married while she seemed destined to be a single-for-lifer.

Kendra chided herself for her silliness. She certainly didn't need a man to complete or fulfill her life. As the youngest tenured professor at Blalock College, she had accomplished more than enough to lead a perfectly full and satisfying life. Maybe God intended for her to stay single. Besides, it wasn't as if she was actively looking for male companionship. She'd had opportunities for dates. But the pickings were somewhat slim in this small town. She'd dated a few men; other invitations she politely declined due to a complete lack of interest on her part. But nobody had ignited sparks. Was she too choosy? Perhaps. But deep down, she wanted her pulse to race and her insides to flutter when she thought of her true love, whoever he might be. Or maybe she was mixing up her expectations with a bad case of a stomach virus. The symptoms were fairly similar, other than one left you feeling euphoric, while the other left you wishing you were dead. Come to think of it, true love could leave a person wishing she were dead, too. But was it too much to ask for ooey-gooey, happily-ever-after love like in romance novels? Or in Ben and Darcy's relationship, which seemed as idyllic as any love story?

Get a grip on yourself, Kendra. The sensible voice in her head tried to rein in the ridiculous feelings that had come over her simply from entering a driveway, at the end of which sat the nearly hundred-year-old ranch house built by Ben's grandfather, where Ben and Darcy lived happily ever after. Kendra needed her brain to focus on the myriad of practical items on her to-do list—first and foremost of which was getting through the reception tonight for her graduate students.

She pulled her car up to the side of the house and turned off the engine, half-expecting to see Darcy come out to meet her. When no one appeared, Kendra exited the car and looked around, finally walking up to the back door.

Hmm, that's funny. The back door always stood open. She knocked and waited. Nothing. Frowning, she backed away from the door and picked her way carefully toward the barn, which sat a good hundred yards away from the house. Maybe they were cleaning out the stalls of the dozen or so horses that grazed in the spacious paddock just outside the barn.

Kendra's expensive heels didn't exactly do well on this turf as they sank into the soft, moist dirt. If she'd only known she would be tramping across this unlevel, unpaved ground, she would have changed clothes before heading straight out in her professional attire. But she had been in a hurry and hadn't counted on having to traipse to the barn. She stopped to pat the noses of a few curious horses who had wandered over to the fence to investigate the visitor. Although more comfortable around the animals than she had been a short while ago, she still felt a little overwhelmed by their size and strength. When she neared the door to the barn, the soft nickering of another horse, accompanied by a low, male voice, reached her ears.

"Ben?" she called out, as she stepped inside,

kicking mud from her spiked heels.

A man standing with his back to her startled, knocking off a mug of coffee that had been resting on stacked hay bales next to where he had been placing a bridle on a horse. He jumped back as the black liquid landed in the straw at his feet, splashing over his boots and splattering his jeans. He turned, flinging coffee from his hand and wiping his hand on his pants. The horse he had been saddling up jerked back in surprise, as well.

It wasn't Ben. A man she had never seen before at the ranch stood glaring at her with intense dark eyes.

Kendra's hand flew to her mouth. "Oh, I'm so sorry. I didn't mean to surprise you."

"Who are you?" he asked gruffly.

She took a tentative step toward him. "I'm Kendra Clark. I'm a friend of Ben and Darcy's." She debated briefly, then extended a hand.

He stared at her for a moment, then, with one corner of his mouth turning down, said, "I'd shake your hand, but I have hot coffee all over mine."

Kendra's eyes widened. "Oh, I'm so sorry," she repeated. "Did you get burned?"

He bent to retrieve the mug and mumbled, "I'll live." He walked past her out of the barn, forcing her to trot after him, trying not to get her heels stuck in the mud again. Setting his mug in the outdoor sink, he muttered, "Couldn't find my thermos. I knew I shouldn't have brought a mug out to the barn. Serves me right." With his back still facing her, he ran water over his hand and said, "Ben and Darcy aren't here."

"What time do you expect them back?" Kendra said, looking at her watch.

The man dried his hands on an old towel hanging from a nail above the sink. "A couple of days."

"*Days*?" Darcy had specifically told Kendra she could come by and borrow her punch bowl for the reception tonight. Had Darcy told her she would be going out of town? Kendra couldn't recall Darcy mentioning it. Still, it was Kendra's fault for leaving everything until the last minute. She should have picked up the punch bowl earlier in the week.

The man turned and leaned against the sink, scrutinizing her with an uncomfortable glower. "Yeah. They had a chance to take off for a couple of days. They didn't have a honeymoon."

Kendra nodded and bit her lower lip. She knew there hadn't been an opportunity for a honeymoon. Ben and Darcy deserved whatever little time they could steal away together. Kendra only wished they had let her know. But, in Darcy's defense, she probably thought Kendra had found another bowl somewhere else since Kendra hadn't gotten back to her. Now where was Kendra supposed to get a punch bowl at this late hour?

"So, what did you want?" The man's brusque tone jolted Kendra out of her churning thoughts.

"I don't suppose you know where Ben and Darcy keep their punch bowl, do you?" Kendra's brows raised in expectant hope.

He peered at her like she had suddenly sprouted horns from her head.

Kendra ducked her chin and pushed out a cheerless laugh. "No, of course you don't. Silly question." She turned to go. "I'm sorry to have bothered—"

"Can't say as I do." The man blew out a long breath. "But you can come in and look for it if you want." He readjusted his Stetson on his head and gestured for her to precede him to the house.

She stopped in her tracks, her mouth forming an "O." Then the tips of her lips curled into a grateful smile. "Thanks. I would appreciate that."

Kendra felt his eyes on her as she tottered across the rough ground in her unsuitable shoes. She stopped at the back door and waited while he produced a key and unlocked the door. Then he motioned for her to enter, as he followed.

Kendra stopped in the middle of the huge kitchen. She loved this room with its wide plank floors, high arched ceiling letting in natural light through twin skylights, and the woodsy smell of pine. It put her spartan little kitchen to shame. But what she didn't love right now, as she stood gazing around, was the endless number of cupboards. Where should she start? She turned to the man, who had stopped just inside the door, waiting with his hands on his hips. He obviously wasn't going to help, so she started opening one oak cabinet after another. Feeling somewhat like a guilty intruder going through her friends' personal space, she filled the uncomfortable silence in the room with endless chatter as she searched.

"I shouldn't have left this to the last minute, but I had so many other things to do," she said as she bent to peruse the contents of the cabinet next to the sink. "I wish I hadn't been put in charge of this reception. Things like this always make me so nervous. I'm afraid I'll forget something important." She straightened up and reached for the cabinet above her head. "But I guess since the reception is for my graduate students, it only makes sense for me to host it." She huffed out a self-conscious laugh. "Still, wouldn't you think a reception would fall under the job description of a secretary or something?"

He didn't reply, which only made her more nervous, and her words came out faster. "Not that I think the job is beneath me or anything like that, and it isn't as if my secretary hasn't helped. She's been wonderful. I just didn't want to ask her to take on more responsibility." Kendra slammed the cabinet door louder than she'd intended as she moved to the next one. "It's just that I've never had to organize something like this before. I don't know why I'm so worried about something so unimportant in the big scheme of things. Not that a reception for my graduate students is unimportant, I didn't mean to imply that. They deserve recognition. They've worked hard."

Having exhausted all the cabinets within reach, she looked around and spied a step stool sitting against the wall. His eyes followed her as she pulled it next to the sink to access the upper cabinets. Again, although not looking at him, she could feel his eyes on her as she gingerly climbed onto the first step, trying to keep her tight skirt from riding up too high. Heat rose in her face, and she knew it accentuated her pale complexion. Why hadn't she taken the time to change clothes? Well, it was perfectly reasonable why she hadn't changed before coming here. She hadn't expected to be teetering on a step ladder in her professional attire. But she wished the taciturn man standing unhelpfully by the door wouldn't make her feel so uneasy.

Kendra raised another tentative leg, hiking her tight skirt slightly above her knee to bend it, and climbed onto the second step. She probably should have kicked off her shoes before attempting this ill-advised maneuver. She rummaged around in the top cabinet. "Nope, don't see it in here, either." She turned and partially faced him. "Oh, I guess I didn't tell you. I'm a professor of biology at Blalock." Now why had she felt the need to tell him that little piece of information? He certainly could care less. She rattled on. "I have three graduate students who are finishing their master's degrees. That's why I'm giving this reception. Well, it wasn't my idea," she continued, as she stretched to examine the cabinet next to the one she'd just inspected. "The dean suggested it would be a good idea and . . . oh! I think I see it."

She went up on tiptoe while trying to kick her other leg out for balance. Her arm strained to grasp the edge of the bowl. The fleeting thought went through her head that she would have been better off to climb down and move the ladder over, but she was so close. Just as her fingers brushed the bowl, her foot slipped. As if in slow motion, she felt her body tumbling, landing against something firm and solid.

IF YOU LIKE ANIMAL STORIES, READ ON
FOR AN EXCERPT FROM
DON'T BITE THE DOCTOR
by
Ellen Fannon
CHAPTER ONE

"I haven't had this much fun since we neutered the squirrel!" I laughed, leaning against the sink, trying to catch my breath.

"Oh, I forgot about that!" Kelly, my long-time technician, laughed with me.

Cara, a second technician, looked up from the phone she cradled against her shoulder. "Wait. You actually neutered a *squirrel?*"

I shrugged. "You know me. I'll neuter anything." Well, except for that pig a few weeks ago. But that was from my firmly entrenched PTSD from my first and only pig neuter in veterinary school, rather than true unwillingness to perform castration surgery. It's a long story.

"Why would you neuter a squirrel?" Cara persisted.

"It belonged to someone who kept it as a pet," Kelly answered. "Remember how it got loose and we chased it all over the surgery room?"

"That was quite a challenge." I smiled at the memory.

Squirrels, it seems, can not only climb trees, they can climb walls. And ceilings. And they are *fast*! They do not corner well, as opposed to other pets with which I am more experienced. This little bugger zinged over our heads, under our feet, and up and down the walls, leaving a trail of upended equipment and surgical supplies in his wake.

"Catching him in midair was pure luck." I didn't like to brag, but I had made an impressive squirrel interception if I did say so myself. As the creature sprang from one surgery wall to the opposite side of the room, I reached up and fortuitously nabbed it at just the right second, like a squirrel flyball. Even more fortuitous was the fact I happened to have a towel in my hand and didn't suffer sharp incisor teeth embedded into my sensitive palm from a panicked rodent who was not too keen on parting with his nuts. Pun intended.

Until today, I hadn't seen an animal with moves like that. Then came Sadie. It wasn't as if I didn't *know* Sadie. For years, I'd had the dubious pleasure of chasing her down in the cat room of the no-kill pet rescue shelter where it was Sadie's fate to live out her nine lives because nobody in their right mind would ever adopt her. Or get near her, provided, of course, that were possible, which it wasn't. Because I am such an accommodating soul, I made the three or four visits a year to the shelter to vaccinate the cats so the unpaid staff didn't have to load them up in crates and truck them to the clinic.

I always saved Sadie until last. That's because I could generally round up and capture everybody else on the list who needed vaccinating. Granted, some were easier than others, but vaccinating Sadie invariably posed a challenge. She would sense me looking at her and race out the doggy door to the screened-in catio (cat patio) and back into the main cat room before I could react. All I ever saw of her was a gray blur. I had to bide my time, waiting until she lit on one of the overhead ledges, then climb gingerly onto a flimsy plastic chair, hoping Sadie felt trapped and wouldn't bolt—or the chair that was not designed for standing wouldn't topple over with me on it.

Sometimes it worked. But more often than not, I had to chase her outside, inside, up on a chair, down off the chair, back outside, up on a chair, down off the chair, back inside . . . well, you get the drift, while the volunteer assigned to me largely stood by helpless. This is why I get paid the big bucks. Hah, who am I kidding? I never charged for my time at the shelter. Eventually, Sadie would freeze in one place and this was when my several years of expertise and quick reflexes came into play. Not to mention luck. I usually had one chance at getting this done. With lightning speed, I would reach out and snatch her by the nape of her neck, praying for a good grip the first time. If I missed, it would either be another ten minutes of playing "chase Sadie," or I would be the recipient of Sadie's quick teeth or razor-sharp claws. With the other hand, I would impale her with the needle in some vague area of hopefully-nothing-anatomically-important, and wa-lah! Done. For another year!

On Sadie vaccination days, the uncomfortable thought always reared its ugly head in the alarmist region of my brain, *I dread the day Sadie gets sick and I have to actually get my hands on her.* I generally managed to push this troublesome thought into the easily forgotten corner of my mind where I wouldn't have to deal with it. Besides, I'm an optimist. I figured a lot of things could happen before that day ever came, such as getting hit by a bus, moving to Africa, or the shelter firing me—well, that's unlikely, since I do their work for free—and I wouldn't have to deal with Sadie if and when that day came.

That's why when Arlene, the cat coordinator at the shelter, called a few weeks ago and said Sadie was drooling excessively and would I mind coming by the shelter to look at her, my heart plummeted.

"Well, I don't mind," I told her. "But *looking at Sadie* is probably the best I can hope for. If you want me to actually examine her, you'll need to find some way of getting her to the clinic because there's no way I can do that without sedating her." *Yeah, good luck with that.*

Arlene agreed, and once again, I pushed Sadie back into the cobwebbed area of my cluttered brain and forgot about her; that is until the day some brave volunteer managed to get her into a carrier and present her at the clinic. To make matters worse, it wasn't my day off.

www.ingramcontent.com/pod-product-compliance
Lightning Source LLC
Chambersburg PA
CBHW060304310726
48976CB00007B/2209
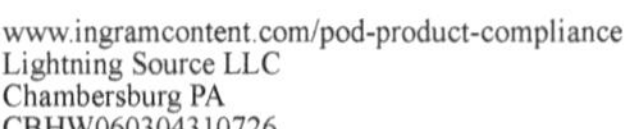